A HARVESTING SERIES NOVELLA

WITCH WOOD

MELANIE KARSAK

Published by Clockpunk Press
PO Box 560367
Rockledge, FL 32956-0367

Clockpunk Press
Cover art by Quirky Bird
Editing by Becky Stephens Editing
Book design by Inkstain Interior Book Designing

for Carrie

WITCH WOOD

THE WITCHING HOUR COLLECTION

CHAPTER ONE

THE AURA AROUND MRS. DELANEY had faded from vibrant green to dull, sludge-colored green-brown as the last class of the day wore down to its end. Despite the fact she was still standing at the blackboard lecturing, a patient smile on her face, her energy told another tale: she was about to drop. She turned and jotted some notes on the board. I noticed that the chalk tray had left a white line of chalk across the back of her black skirt in a none-too-flattering spot. I hoped the boys wouldn't notice.

"Witch," a whisper came from behind me. "Amelia...hey, witchy woman."

Nate must have gotten bored. Instead of just texting like everyone else, he was about to launch into his tired barrage. I ignored him, hoping it would dissuade him, but pretending he didn't exist rarely phased him. He was the glowing center of his own universe. Other people's perceptions didn't matter to him.

"Ah-meel-ya," he chanted. "Witch, why don't you let me put some sex in your hex."

I looked at Zoey who was sitting beside me in the next row and rolled my eyes.

I was so over with this day. With half the class out sick, Nate—hipster extraordinaire and total douche—was running low on girls to hit on. Jenna and Sam, who sat behind Zoey and me, usually acted as a buffer. For some reason I never understood, they both liked Nate's attention. But they were both absent. If I didn't know it would come back on me tenfold, I'd cast a spell to silence his disgusting mouth. But I was a good witch, Glinda without the bubble, and I had no business casting hexes.

"Rhyming? I didn't know you were that smart, Nate," Zoey, who was less patient than me, shot back.

"Logan, you smell fish?" Nate whispered to Logan who sat beside him. "Zoey, close your legs."

Out of the corner of my eye, I glanced at Logan. A newcomer, Logan had moved to Brighton at the beginning of the year. I could see him and the soft purple and indigo glow that always surrounded him.

Logan shifted uncomfortably then frowned at Nate. "Don't be a dick. Sorry, Zoey. Nate doesn't have any manners."

Nate laughed. "Whatever. Oh, Edward Cullen, you're such a gentleman," Nate teased him. "Like Zoey and Amelia even matter."

Since he first started school, Logan had always lingered on the outskirts of Nate's tribe. It seemed that he wasn't actually a jerk like Nate and his friends. And then there was the other thing about him that set him apart. He was an A student, too busy actually paying attention to what Mrs. Delaney had to say in class to be a jerk. And today, Mrs. Delaney's lecture focused on Shakespeare's *Macbeth*.

I scanned around the classroom. Of the less than a dozen students in class, half of them were on their phones. Mrs. Delaney was explaining—mainly to the board at this point—the meaning of the witches' chant in the play.

"Hey, Amelia, can you brew me a love potion to get Jenna to suck me off?" Nate whispered.

"Could you be any more disrespectful?" Logan chided just as Mrs. Delaney, who'd finally had enough, turned and faced the class.

"In the back...shush. Now, someone tell me, which goddess is said to have been insulted by this play? Anyone actually paying attention? Which goddess cursed Shakespeare's work?"

I glanced back at Logan through my long, wheat-colored hair. Most days we would race to be the first to answer but not today. The last thing I wanted to do was draw more attention to the fact that I knew about witchcraft. While I'd been practicing Wicca since I was thirteen, the year I stumbled across a used copy of *Wicca: A Guide for the Solitary Practitioner* by Scott Cunningham in a used bookstore, I'd always been different. Being Wiccan meant promoting peace, protecting my environment, and feeling at one with the Great Mother. The idiot behind me, however, didn't know the difference between a devil worshipper—which I was not—and Samantha from *Bewitched*. And I wasn't in the mood to explain to him that I only performed good magic, earth and healing magic.

"Zoey?" Mrs. Delaney called.

"Sorry, Mrs. D. I zoned."

"Nate?"

"Pass."

"Of course. Amelia?"

"I…" I began, then glanced up at her. Mrs. Delaney was, by far, my favorite teacher. In the ninth grade, she'd introduced me to Madame Knightly, the owner of Witch Wood Estate, whom I took care of three nights a week and on weekends. I was eternally grateful for the job. I'd already stashed away enough cash to pay for my first year of college. Just the week before, I'd gotten my invite to Claddagh-Basel College for an admission interview. It was really happening. I was going to study Psychology at one of the best schools in the country. And all that had happened because Mrs. Delaney, who kept crystals on her desk and wore a medicine bag around her neck, had seen something in me that the others had ignored. "Hecate," I said then. "Hecate is the dark goddess named in the play. The editor's notes said that Shakespeare got the Weird Sisters' chant from a real witch and that Hecate cursed the play because of it. Some productions remove Hecate just to get rid of the jinx."

"Exactly. Well done," she said with a smile then glanced up at the clock. My eyes followed hers.

Thank the Goddess, the day was done.

"All right, class. Please review King's essay on the use of symbolism in the play and compose a two-page summary."

"You're kidding, right? School's gonna be closed next week," Brant, a football player, grumbled from the front row—where his coach had mandated he sit.

"Are you really asking me that?" Mrs. Delaney replied, frowning at him. I could see her aura growing even darker, sadder. She really needed to get out of here. "Thus far, they haven't announced a closure for Monday. Yes, we're the last school in the county still open. But still, *read, write*. It won't hurt you."

A moment later, the bell rang.

"Whatever," Brant grumbled under his breath then headed out the door.

"Let's get out of here," Zoey said. Rising, she stuffed her book into her backpack.

Nate pushed past. "Sorry," he said as he pretended to trip, banging his crotch against Zoey's butt.

"Screw you, Nate. Do that again, and I'll have Amelia cast a spell to rot it off," Zoey warned him.

I couldn't help but laugh.

"Freaks," Nate said, glaring from Zoey to me, but I couldn't help but see the look of fear cross his eyes. He wasn't sure if I could really do something like that. In the end, it was better that he didn't know I would never, ever practice dark magic. Harm none and do as you will, that is the motto of Wiccans. I wasn't looking for trouble to come back to me.

I dug into my bag. "Almost forgot," I said, handing Zoey as small, amber-colored vial.

"What's this?" she asked, looking at the bottle.

"Eucalyptus and rosemary oil," I replied. "Put it in your bath or on a cloth to inhale it. It helps keep your respiratory system clear. Should help ward off the cold going around."

"Thanks," she said, opening the bottle to take a sniff. "Ooh, my nose is burning." She giggled.

Logan walked up behind Zoey and me. "Hey, Amelia… you're organizing the Halloween dance?" he asked.

His dark hair fell over his black-rimmed glasses. He pushed back then paused to arrange his scarf inside his heavy winter pea coat. For autumn, it was terribly cold and the reports of flu were already out of control. No wonder he was bundled up. His honey-colored eyes crinkled in the corners when he smiled at me. My knees went soft.

"Uh, yeah. We've just started planning. We're still working on a theme."

"Ms. Flynn says I need another extracurricular. Mind if I help?"

"If you want," I replied, trying to play it cool when inside I was screaming like a tween at a Justin Bieber concert. "The next meeting is Tuesday at six. We meet down at Studio," I said, referring to the local coffee bar where Zoey worked. When I wasn't at Witch Wood, I spent all my time there, especially when Mom was at work. The last thing I wanted was to be penned up at home with my stepdad, Larry.

"Great. I'll be there," he replied then looked at the vial Zoey was holding. "So, a white witch? For real?" he asked.

I nodded. "Yeah, I know, it's weird, but, it's just, you know…" I said, trailing off. *It's just what, Amelia? You're a witch. Own it.*

Logan raised an eyebrow at me.

"Yes, I'm a white witch. I do healing and stuff. All-natural lifestyle. That kind of thing."

"Dude?" Nate called to Logan from the door.

Logan grinned at me. "You do protection spells? I need one. My sister got that flu. She was puking all night, and I hate being sick."

"I do," I said then arched an eyebrow at him. "You really want me to—"

"Go for it. Please."

"Okay then. This will just take a minute." I closed my eyes, inhaled deeply, and then tried to envision the energy field, the aura, surrounding him. I envisioned white light passing from me to him, surrounding him with a glowing white energy that would protect him. With my mind's eye, I inscribed this light with a protection rune that glowed with glimmering blue light. In my mind, I chanted:

"Goddess Mother, may this light protect him from all harm.
May this light keep away all illness.
May this light keep him safe from darkness.
May this light bring him peace.
So mote it be.
With thanks, I pray thee."

I exhaled then opened my eyes. I could still see the white light shimmering all around him. "Done," I said then smiled.

Logan grinned. "That easy? Cool. I feel much safer now. Thanks, Amelia. See you next week," he said then headed toward the door.

"What were you doing?" Nate asked Logan.

Logan shrugged off the question, not answering, and they headed down the hall.

"God, I'm crushing on him so hard right now. That was awesome. You should have seen how he was looking at you. *Lust*!" she said, emphasizing the last word in sing-song. "But I don't get it. Why in the hell does he hang around with Nate?" Zoey asked as she pulled her long black and mermaid blue tresses out of the back of her jacket. They tumbled down her back to her waist.

"Their parents are connected or something," I replied. "Brianna and Brian said their dads work together. And he's new. He doesn't know better yet. You heard him call Nate out. He's not like them."

"Well, he's definitely into you," Zoey said as we moved toward the door.

"Na. I'm just a curiosity."

"Did you even register what just happened? All guys secretly dig the weird girls, but I think Logan actually likes you."

"You think?" My heart slammed in my chest.

"Guess you'll find out Tuesday."

"So mote it be," I said with a wink.

Zoey laughed.

"Amelia?" Mrs. Delaney called as Zoey and I headed toward the door. "Will you see Madame Knightly this weekend?"

I nodded.

"Be sure to wish her well for me."

"Will do," I said with a smile.

"Oh, and Amelia, don't cast in class," she said with a laugh.

I smiled at her. "Okay, Mrs. D. Get some rest this weekend. You...you feeling okay?"

"Just run down," she said then tapped her medicine bag. "We're going out to the reservation this weekend to see my husband's parents. They usually do powwow this time of year. School year started rough..." she said, her voice trailing off.

Rough. Yes, her aura definitely agreed. "Rest up. We'll see you Monday."

She nodded and waved us off.

Zoey and I then turned and headed down the hallway toward

the exit. Over the loudspeaker, Coach Nestor was making announcements. "Tonight's basketball game against the Laughlin Vikings is cancelled. Laughlin High School has been closed due to the flu outbreak. A reminder from the nurse's office, please stay home if you are experiencing flu-like symptoms. Call the attendance line to report any absences. Make ample use of hand sanitizer to avoid spreading illnesses."

"Have a good weekend, Miss Beatrice," Zoey called as our lanky, blonde-haired biology teacher rushed past balancing her school bag, a coffee cup, and her cell phone. She was texting furiously.

"You too, Zoey...Amelia. I'll see you at Studio Saturday night. Allen and I got tickets for the play at the theater. If they don't cancel. Later, girls," she said then raced down the hall.

I couldn't help but notice that half the male teachers and male students turned to watch her go past. She was gorgeous, that was certain, like the kind of hot teacher you always saw getting fired because she was secretly a bikini model in her spare time. Her boyfriend was the town celebrity, a PGA golfer or something. I didn't have her for class this year, but I'd taken advanced biology with her junior year. She was wicked smart. I must have wondered a hundred times why she was teaching at a high school.

"God, if I could get the flu maybe I could drop these last ten pounds before the Halloween dance. My dieselpunk outfit would look so hot if I wasn't so flabby," Zoey said absently as we headed out into the crisp, autumn air.

With her athletic frame from playing softball, Zoey was hardly flabby. "That's gross. Just stop eating fries like they're a food group."

"They aren't?" she asked with a wink. "Don't go hippie on me, Miss perfect-boho-more-lithe-than-air figure because I am one with mineral water and acorns. Figure out what you're going to go dressed up as yet?"

"I was thinking Harley Quinn. Not sure yet."

"Well, I'm sure you and your date will come up with something."

"Date?"

"Logan, of course, when he asks you on Tuesday. Don't say no."

"Stop shipping."

"You know you want him."

"Whatever."

When we reached the front steps, we stopped so Zoey could dig through her bag for her van keys. I eyed the parking lot. Logan was getting into a car with Nate, Katie, and Brad. The popular crowd. Not my crowd. I looked around for Brian and Brianna. Their car was gone. I hadn't seen them since first period. Had they gone home sick?

Zoey finally pulled out her keys. "Sure you don't want me to drop you off?"

"Na. I haven't had enough bonding time with the acorns today."

Zoey laughed. "Fine. But you want me to pick you up at Witch Wood Monday morning?"

"Please."

"Hugs," she said then, pulling me into an embrace. "Don't overdose on too much *Matlock* and Werther's candies this weekend. And don't get sick. Call me, okay?"

"Dead spot, remember? I'll try…if the rotary phone is working.

It's been acting strange." Strange was an understatement. Since last weekend the old rotary phone kept ringing, but there was never anyone on the line...just static and strange tinny sounds.

Zoey nodded. "Okay, I'm gonna be late for work. Later, babes," Zoey called then flounced down the steps toward her van.

I took a deep breath, inhaling the crisp autumn wind. This weekend marked the feast of Mabon, the harvest festival, and I was planning to spend it with the one person who understood me best, Madame Knightly. Of course, before I could run off to the haven of Witch Wood Estate, I had to make a stop at the place where I hated to be most...home.

CHAPTER TWO

"WHAT DO YOU MEAN YOU'RE headed back for another shift?" I could hear my stepfather's voice rising from inside as soon as I stepped onto the porch. Part of me debated whether or not to go in. The last thing I needed was to walk into yet another of their arguments. I cursed myself for not thinking ahead. Next Friday, I'd pack everything in the morning and leave it in Zoey's car.

Moving as quietly as I could, I opened the front door and slipped off my shoes in the foyer.

"What am I supposed to do? The hospital is packed. They are sending people over from Grand Falls. The flu that's got half the country knocked out is bad over there. Everyone who isn't sick is working, not just me," my mother replied. I realized then that she was in the shower. It was just like my stepdad to pick an argument when she couldn't get away.

"And how am I supposed to know that's where you're really going? You've been working late all week. You could be anywhere. With anyone."

"Turn on the news. This flu is out of hand. People have been throwing up on me all day. Stop being ridiculous."

I'd just turned the corner to slip into my bedroom when I heard my stepdad launch himself from the recliner and thunder down the hall toward the bathroom. In that moment, I was simultaneously glad and horrified to be caught unexpected in the middle of their fight. On the one hand, whatever might have happened next wouldn't happen because I was there. On the other hand, I was there…and I knew that my stepdad never let my mom talk to him like that. For maybe the millionth time, I wondered why my mother put up with him. It wasn't like he contributed anything to our family, and the charming man he'd been when he first swept her off her feet had vanished about four seconds after they'd gotten married. The sweet guy who'd brought me stuffed animals was replaced with a slug who'd practically glued himself to the recliner from which he spent his day shouting profanities at sports teams. I couldn't even remember the last time he had a job.

"When did you get here?" he said, jumping sideways when he almost ran into me. The smell of cheap beer and sweat emanated from him. "Amelia's here," he screamed to my mother.

"Honey, I have to go back to the hospital. Are you headed to Witch Wood?"

"Yeah, I'm just getting my things."

"Lasagna in the fridge if you want it. Mushroom."

"Thank you," I called then stood in the hallway between Larry and the door to the bathroom. A nonverbal showdown, I simply stood and waited.

"Working this weekend too, eh?" he said finally.

"Yes." *I am…Mom is…what about you, you lazy piece of garbage?*

"You keeping your grades up?"

"Yes." *Like you care.*

Realizing I wasn't going to move, he grunted then turned and headed back to the kitchen for another beer.

I slipped into my room and packed up my clothes, books, and laptop. I had everything I needed to escape the hellhole that was home. I slid off my long gypsy skirt and pulled on a pair of jeans, sweatshirt, and boots. From the back of my closet, I dug out my winter jacket. It smelled dusty, vaguely like the perfume I wore last winter, and…mint? I remembered then that I'd poured mouthwash on it last spring. I needed to send it for dry cleaning. Next week. I would need it at Witch Wood over the weekend. Madame Knightly rarely heated the upper floors of the massive old estate. Since she couldn't easily get upstairs anymore, there wasn't any use. She'd taken to living entirely on the first floor of the old mansion. More and more, I worried about leaving her when I went off to college the following year…her *and* my mom.

I shoved my heavy coat into my backpack, then grabbed my witch's bag. The bag, which contained my oils, herbs, and magical tools, came in handy at Witch Wood. There was always wild herbs to be cut. Last weekend I'd found a bunch of lavender growing wild in what must have been the kitchen herb garden—once upon a time. I'd pressed it into a nice oil. All packed up, I headed toward the back of the house.

"Mom?" I called.

"Here," she said then clicked on the hairdryer.

I opened the bathroom door slowly. "You decent?"

"As I'm gonna get," she replied.

The steam in the bathroom was so thick I could barely

breathe. Mom was wrapped in a massive beach towel, blow drying the water from her thick, brown hair.

"Headed out now?" she asked.

I nodded.

Mom clicked off the dyer and set it on the pink porcelain counter. Larry hated our 1950s bathroom with its pink sink and tub and black and white tiles, but Mom and I loved its faded charm.

"Ugh...I have a migraine. Will you do the thing before you go? Pretty please? For me?" she asked, batting her lashes and giving me her sweetest puppy eyes.

"Sure," I replied.

Mom sat down sideways on the toilet, and I sat on the side of the tub behind her.

"I took four pain killers but nothing is touching this headache."

"You shouldn't go back to work if you feel sick."

"I just need a cigarette," she whispered. Mom never smoked with Larry around. Despite all his vices, he hated smoking. He and Mom never agreed on the issue so Mom took to smoking in secret. Larry always lost his temper when he caught her. I shuddered to think of the time I found her crying in a rumpled heap in the corner of their bedroom. I hadn't seen the fight, but I'd seen the aftermath. Mom never talked about what happened, but I'd noticed her shirt was ripped, her cheek red, and her pack of cigarettes shredded in a messy heap on their bed. The irony was, Mom hadn't smoked until Larry came into the picture.

"Okay, try to be still and quiet," I told her.

I inhaled deeply and focused, squinting my eyes so I could see

15

the halo of color around her more closely. Usually her aura was a mix of pastel blues, pinks, and purples. Today, however, black energy circled her head.

"It *is* a bad one," I said.

"Told you."

Rubbing my hands together, I felt my own energy grow. My hands were covered in bright white light. Focusing, I penetrated my hands into her aura and began pulling away the dark strings of energy.

Uncontrollably, she whimpered.

I worked and worked, releasing the darkness that surrounded her back into the air, banishing it from us. But it made for hard work. The blackness was sticky, like it didn't want to let go. It kept trying to reattach itself to her over and over again. Weird. Focusing hard, I finally pulled all the bad energy away. It lifted through the ceiling and dissipated. After about ten minutes or so, long enough for the steam to disappear, I'd cleaned off the last of the darkness.

I pulled my hands back then rose. "Feel better?" I asked her.

Mom opened her eyes. "You sure you're my daughter? I've never understood how you do that."

"Sure you do. You do the same thing, you just don't realize it. Healing touch, remember? Why do you think everyone tells you that you're the best nurse at the hospital?" I replied then went to the sink and washed my hands, imagining any lingering darkness washing away.

"Because I take all the extra shifts, cover them when they need time off, bake cookies, you know, that stuff?" my mom replied with a laugh, then wrapped her arms around me. "Love you, baby girl. Thank you."

"Love you too," I said, lifting her hands and kissing them one after the other.

"What in the hell are you two doing in there?" Larry shouted from the living room.

Mom rolled her eyes. "Amelia got her period," she yelled back.

We giggled quietly.

I heard Larry mutter, but he didn't ask anything else.

"See you Tuesday night, right?" Mom asked, pushing a strand of hair away from my face.

I nodded.

"Okay then," she said then turned back to the mirror.

I looked at her again. Her aura…it still looked strange. Dark colors zipped all around her usually placid, pastel-colored glow. "So many people are getting sick. Be careful, okay?"

Mom shrugged then started pulling a brush through her long hair. "I'll be all right. I've had the flu shot and a shot for just about everything else under the moon. Wait, did you go to Doctor Darling's for your flu shot? I didn't see an invoice come from the insurance company."

"And that's my cue to leave," I said with a grin as I opened the bathroom door.

"Amelia!"

"I have my echinacea, and vegetarians never get sick."

"Seriously. You didn't get it?

"No, and I won't need it. You know I'm right. I never get sick. Clean living, Mom. Try it some time."

"And give up my Whoppers? Never."

17

I rolled my eyes. "That's not even meat. Do you know that they put—"

Raising her hand, she silenced me. "Don't tell me. I don't want to know."

"No, you don't."

"Have a good weekend, honey. And thank you again," she said, motioning to her head. "Love you."

"Love you too." I waved to her then headed back out. Pulling on my backpack, I headed toward the front door. Larry had gone back to sitting in the living room watching a rerun of *America's Funniest Home Videos*.

"And just who is going to take care of me? Everyone around here will be busy wiping old people's asses this weekend. I guess I'm just supposed to sit here by myself," Larry half-heartedly grumbled at me, but he got distracted when a little boy on the TV shot a mile-long booger out of his nose. He laughed loudly.

I rolled my eyes then headed out the front door only to half-trip over my neighbor, Mrs. Sommers, who was standing on the porch.

"Jesus, Mary, and Joseph. You scared me half to death," Mrs. Sommers exclaimed. "Of course, *I'm* standing on *your* porch." She laughed loudly.

"Sorry," I replied. "I was just heading out. Can I help you with something?"

"I was wondering if Larry was home? Bill's been laid up with the flu the past two days, and I can't get the furnace lit. They say it might freeze tonight."

"Larry?" I called back into the house.

"What? I thought you left," my stepdad grumbled in reply.

"Mrs. Sommers is on the porch. She's looking for you."

I heard him grunt as he lowered the leg rest on the recliner, complaining bitterly under his breath about "that annoying old bag" as he made his way to the door. I said a silent prayer that Mrs. Sommers hadn't heard him. Not wanting to be there a moment longer, I stepped around Mrs. Sommers and headed down the stairs.

"Mrs. Sommers! Let me guess, you made me some seven-layer cookies?"

My neighbor, who, as far as I could remember, had lived beside me all my life, laughed uncomfortably. I had some vague memory of her and her husband attending one of my dad's birthday parties. I could almost envision Dad on the front porch grilling while Mrs. Sommers chatted with him over a massive bowl of potato salad. Was it real or my imagination? After all, I was only five when my dad went off to Afghanistan and never came back. I hardly remembered him anymore.

"Well, actually..." she began, but I headed out of earshot. I didn't want to mess up my memory by inserting Larry into the picture any more than I had already.

My bike, which sat parked under the old oak tree in the front yard, was covered in orange- and gold-colored leaves. The crisp fall air was perfumed with their decaying scent.

I paused and set my hand on the tree. The bark under my hand felt gritty.

"Oak spirit, I honor your transformation. Thank you for your life-giving breath, your acorns, and the strength of your roots. Sacred oak, watcher of the woods, keep my home safe. So mote it be. In thanks, I pray thee."

I felt a strange tingling sensation. My whole hand felt like it was buzzing with electricity. And with my mind's eye, I could see the glow of amber-colored light pulsating from the old oak, touching the violet-colored aura that emanated from me. I felt our energies touch and warm energy—like the sensation you get when you're shocked by static fresh from the dryer—passed between us.

I pulled my hand away then guided my bike to the road. Usually the traffic was busy at this time of day. Where was everyone? I peddled down Maple Lane and onto Fifth Street. A lone truck swerved around me, the driver shouting something incomprehensible out the window. Drivers always seemed to have some odd contempt for bicyclists, like we reminded them that they should be biking or walking or doing something other than polluting the earth with exhaust fumes. Or, at least, that's what I told myself. I had enough money for a car, I just didn't want to spend it. I needed that cash for the great escape from the no man's land Brighton had become. One day, I'd be far away from here, living the life of my dreams. I couldn't wait for that day to come.

CHAPTER
THREE

IT TOOK ME ALMOST AN hour to bike from my house to Witch Wood Estate which was located on the outskirts of town. While rumors abounded about the name of the old estate, Madame Knightly always insisted it was named Witch Wood because of the rowan trees growing on the property. The trees, which lined the wall surrounding the estate, were called by the common name of witch wood. There were whispers, however, that the original Knightly family had moved from Ireland to America to escape religious persecution for their pagan practices. Madame Knightly would just laugh whenever I mentioned it, calling it nonsense. In my heart, I knew Madame Knightly was either not telling the truth or didn't know the truth. There were engravings all around the house that were pagan in origin: ancient Celtic knot work, ogham marks, runes, and symbols for the Father God and Mother Goddess. As well, the statuary that dotted the property depicted old gods. Medicinal and magical herbs grew in every garden. Maybe Madame Knightly didn't know the significance of all the magical things that surrounded her, but I did. And even greater proof of its magical nature was the fact that Witch Wood had a strong aura.

Auras. I'd grown up thinking everyone could see the energy that surrounds all things. It wasn't until the third grade, however, that I learned how wrong my assumption was.

"Amelia, why do you always draw colors around people?" Mrs. Haphousen, my third grade art teacher, had asked.

Her question confused me. "Because there *are* colors around people."

"No, there isn't."

"Sure there is. You have a little halo of orange all around you. And I think you must be sick, because your tummy looks yellow and pink."

Mrs. Haphousen gave me a long, hard look. "Maybe you see those colors, maybe you don't, but other people definitely do not see them. It's the radiance of the Lord you see. It's a special gift to be able to see the Lord's divine light, Amelia."

A few weeks later, Mrs. Haphousen went away on leave. I remember that someone told me later that she was at home taking care of a brand new baby girl. Her replacement teacher, Mister Foote, gave me check-minuses on all my pictures and told me to stop drawing "rainbows" around people. After that, I never colored an aura again.

But I'd never stopped seeing auras. Over the years I tried to help people, to use magical aura healing to clear away the darkness of illness I saw around them. I was actually getting good at it. People always had auras. Places and things often had a glow, but many times it wasn't as vibrant. Witch Wood, however, had a vibe all its own, as big and bright as a living person's. It changed with the seasons, matching the feel of each time of year. And then there was the light and vibration surrounding the gate. The massive old wrought iron gate glowed brightly and had a vibration moving almost beyond perception. There was no doubt in my mind that the gate was enchanted. But why? And by whom?

I stopped just outside the gate where a massive old oak tree grew.

"Grandfather," I said, bowing to the tree. It was, by far, the largest oak in the forest. It was so wide that it would take four people to wrap their arms around it. The energy coming off the tree was strong. In my studies, I had learned that oak trees were considered sacred to the ancient druids. Linked in myth to the ancient Celtic gods, the oak was the most revered tree in the forest.

I hopped off my bike and pushed it up the small lane to the gate. The fence surrounding Witch Wood was made of stone. The gate itself, however, was beautiful wrought iron. The iron had been formed to look like swirling rose vines. The letter W trimmed both gates. I dropped the kickstand on my bike and went to investigate the gate handle. The vibration seemed worse today. I tried twice to catch the handle. It was only on the third attempt that I was able to grab it. It had been moving faster than I could shake from my vision. Weird. Maybe I needed glasses. Or, maybe that borderline anemia was finally catching up with me. Or, maybe…what was the spell on the gate?

I pushed down the handle then opened the gate. It groaned in protest. I went back to retrieve my bike then swung the gate closed again, locking it from the inside. I noticed, as usual, that from the inside the gate looked normal. I loved Witch Wood.

What an odd place…the perfect place for me. I pushed my bike up the driveway toward the massive building.

Witch Wood looked like a traditional English manor home. It was built with gray colored stones taken from the farmland all around Brighton. The tall chimneys, nine in all, were visible above the tree line. The building was six stories in height, and big enough to house more than a hundred people. The faded photos—and the paintings that had come from Ireland before photography—hanging all around the house, showed the Knightly family had been a big one.

The long driveway, which circled upon itself and back out again, led me to the front door. At the center of the drive was a massive fountain shaped like a rowan tree. Water dripped water from its long, metal limbs. Discolored over time, the tree had now faded to the same green hue as the Statue of Liberty. There were more fountains on the property, but many no longer worked or had become overgrown by the untended gardens. I loved the wildness of the grounds. You never knew when you'd run across a statue hiding among the vines. There was a Green Man statue, a harvest goddess, a warrior woman with two dogs, an ancient-looking full-breasted Mother Goddess, and a replica of the Aphrodite of Knidos—that one was my favorite. There was even a hedge maze, not that I'd ever had the chance to try it out.

"Don't go into the maze," Madame Knightly would always warn me whenever I went outside to fetch something. The serious tone in her otherwise light and cordial voice always set me on edge.

"Why not?"

"Oh," she would say, trying to lighten the mood, "there's a trick to it. It's not a regular maze. Finding your way back without help is next to impossible. I'm too old to come fetch you, Amelia. And I might be lost myself in trying. Be a good girl and listen to my words. Stay out."

I gave the front door a hard knock to let her know I was there, just like I always did, then pulled an old wrought-iron key from my pocket. I unlocked the door then leaned hard against the old wooden beast to push it open. The door, decorated with swirling Celtic knots, was heavy enough to ward off a battalion. It had grown sticky with disuse, the hinges squeaking when I pushed them open. There was no way Madame Knightly would ever be able to open it alone, which worried me, because as far as I knew, it was the only door in and out of the house.

"Madame Knightly?" I called, setting the key down on the center drum table. The early evening sunlight shone through the large window above the front door and onto the crystal chandelier overhead. It cast blobs of multi-colored light all around the walls, floor, and ceiling of the circular entryway. The glimmering light sparkled on the mosaic of a massive old oak tree with long, deep roots on the floor.

"Amelia?" Madame Knightly's thin voice called from the direction of the library.

"It's me! TGIF," I called in reply.

I could hear Madame Knightly's laugh. I set my pack down at the foot of the stairs then headed toward the library. As I moved through the west wing of the house, passing through what Madame Knightly always called the ladies' parlor—the gentlemens' parlor was located in the east wing—I noticed that Madame Knightly had pulled out a lot of books from the library. They were stacked *everywhere*, heaped on the floor, lying open on tables, pages marked with dried flowers, handkerchiefs, and old photos. It looked like she'd moved an entire section of the library into the common living quarters. And more than that, Madame Knightly's journal was sitting on her favorite chair. I never pried, but I often saw her taking notes in the old, leather-bound book. From the looks of the words scrawled all over the pages, she'd been taking a lot of notes lately. Under all those books, I saw I had a lot of dusting to do. It was going to be a busy weekend.

I passed through the parlor, then the family room, then turned and followed the hallway down to the massive old library that took up the rest of the west wing. There, I found Madame Knightly standing in front of an old wooden table thumbing through a book. She looked more frail than usual. Her tiny frame, which must have carried less than a hundred pounds, looked lithe. She was, as always, nicely dressed. She wore a lacey green blouse with a high neck and a long spring-green-colored skirt with hand-embroidered pink roses. Her white hair was pulled up into a loose bun, ringlets of curls peeking out here and there. She'd stuck a pencil in the bun for safe-keeping. She was tapping her finger on one of the pages in the book when I entered. Apparently, she'd found what she was looking for.

"Happy weekend," I called cheerfully.

"Amelia, dear," she said, smiling softly as she held out a piece of paper to me. "Would you be so kind as to retrieve this book for me? It's on the balcony, and I didn't want to risk it."

I glanced down at the paper to see a call number scrawled thereon. "Of course," I said, eyeing the narrow balcony overhead. In the back of the library was a spiral staircase that led to the loft above the first floor. There you could find another massive section of books and other curiosities. Small, locked metal cases, figurines, wooden boxes, tinkered contraptions—whose purpose I still didn't know—and other oddities lined the shelves in addition to the old books. I took the paper from Madame Knightly's hand and headed toward the stairs.

"How was school, Amelia?"

I thought back to my exchange with Logan. It had been a pretty great day actually. As long as they didn't close school next week, I might even have a chance talk to him—away from Nate. The idea sent butterflies whomping through my stomach.

"Good," I said as I gripped the wrought iron handrail and started up the spiral staircase. "Mrs. Delaney said to wish you well."

"Oh? How is she?"

How was she? I wasn't sure, really. "She wasn't feeling great. She and her husband are going to the reservation this weekend. He's Seneca, isn't he?"

"Yes," Madame Knightly answered absently.

"They closed Laughlin High. I guess the flu is really bad over there. Half my class was out sick. Mom said the hospital is packed. She's going back tonight. She was bugging me about the flu shot. You get one?" My finger brushed along the spines of the old leather-bound books until I found the book she was looking for. The title was written in Latin.

When Madame Knightly didn't answer, I turned and looked down at her. "Madame Knightly?"

"Sorry, dear. You asked something?" When Madame Knightly looked up at me, she had a strange expression on her usually placid face. And I couldn't help but notice that the soft silver shimmer that always surrounded her looked darker, stormier.

"I'd asked if you'd gotten a flu shot. Madame Knightly, is everything okay?" I asked.

She forced a smile. "Of course, dear. And heavens no, I did not. You didn't, did you?"

"No. I know how to take care of my body." I turned back to the shelf, pulling out the book she'd asked for. "I found the book you wanted," I said, trying to sound chipper, but her fake smile had unnerved me. I'd never seen Madame Knightly perturbed by anything. I headed back down the steps and handed the old book to her.

With a smile, she took the book from my hand and set it aside. On her table, I saw she'd been reading a passage on the bubonic plague. She linked her arm in mine, and turning us, she led us out of the library and back toward the front of the mansion.

"How are your friends, Amelia? Anyone sick? Your mother?"

"Zoey is okay. My mom is working herself to death, but otherwise fine."

Madame Knightly smiled, nodded, and patted my hand.

"What would you like me to work on first? Dusting? Laundry?"

Madame Knightly smiled. "I want you to walk the fence. See if there are any loose rocks that need mended. When I was a girl, we used to plant pumpkins down in the south field. This time of year one or two pumpkins always turns up. Would you see if you can find one for me?"

"Check the fence and look for a…pumpkin?"

"Yes. Thank you, dear. Did you bring a coat? It's getting cold outside."

A pumpkin? "I did," I said, opening up my backpack. I pulled out my coat and my witch's bag. "Oh, speaking of which, would you like me to call Mr. Sanders to have firewood delivered?"

Madame Knightly shook her head. "No need. I had the propane tanks filled."

I was puzzled. Madame Knightly never bothered to get that much fuel. Usually one fireplace was all the two of us needed. The tanks could heat the whole house. I raised an eyebrow at her.

"Off you go...before it gets dark," she said, helping me into my coat. She smiled as she buttoned it up. I strapped by bag bandolier style across my body. "Be careful. And mind you, stay out of the maze."

"Of course," I said, smiling knowingly at her.

Puzzled, I headed outside. I had more than an hour to check the fence and hunt wild pumpkins. More than enough time to finish the job and be back in time for *Matlock*.

CHAPTER
FOUR

THE FALL AIR FELT CRISP. I headed behind the manor, following the pebble-lined path past the broken-down greenhouse, unused tennis courts, overgrown gazing pools whose water had congealed with thick algae, and the wild tangle that the rose garden had become. Part of me suspected Madame Knightly just wanted some privacy to look through the book I'd retrieved. The other part of me wondered if maybe she was just getting nostalgic. I certainly didn't remember seeing any wild pumpkins growing on the property before. Across from the rose garden was the hedge maze. I could just make out the top of an elaborate structure somewhere at its center.

I paused and looked into the maze. It felt…stranger…than usual. Just like the fence, the maze had taken on an odd vibration. A strong wind blew from within, carrying with it the pungent scent of a dead animal. It nearly gagged me.

I covered my hand with my nose then jumped when Madame Knightly's cat, Bastet, appeared at the maze entrance. The black cat, who had glowing, emerald-colored eyes, meowed at me.

"What did you do? Kill a rat in there?"

The cat trotted to my side, rubbed her head on my shin, and then followed behind me as I set off to check the fence. The task was, no doubt, a fool's errand. But I went just in case. Made of stone and wrought iron, and taller than my head, the fence look as sturdy as ever. Not one chink in the old lady's armor was undone.

I headed up the slope to the south field. The sun was beginning to drop low in the sky. I hoped I would have enough time to find what Madame Knightly had asked for.

Bastet ran ahead of me to the pinnacle of the hill.

When I reached the top, I was surprised. The vista below me was alive with the color orange. Pumpkins were growing everywhere. I took a few steps down the slope toward the field, startling a flock of crows that had been picking the shafts of wheat growing among the gourds. The birds cawed in protest and lifted off the ground. Given I was higher than they were, I had to duck when they suddenly came winging toward me. I could hear the thunder of their dark feathers. They complained loudly as they flew overhead.

Bastet hissed and ducked low to the ground.

As they passed over, I was momentarily overcome with dizziness. The cawing voices seemed to call my name as their black shadows passed over me. For a moment, I had a strange vision, seeing myself standing above a group of people who were calling to me, their voices as loud and desperate as the crows' caws. And amongst them, I saw a flash of red—blood.

Bastet meowed loudly once more and wound her way through my legs, causing my eyes to pop open.

I righted myself and looked back. The crows had flown off into the night sky. The fading sunlight was a lovely combination of flaming red, indigo, and magenta colors. The birds appeared like black specks on the watercolor horizon.

"Well, that was weird," I whispered to Bastet who only meowed in reply.

I went to the edge of the pumpkin patch and bent low to grab one of the smaller pumpkins. From my witch's bag, I pulled out my makeup case. Inside was my boline, a small, sickle-shaped knife which I used during magical ceremonies and to cut herbs. Witch Wood had loads of magical herbs growing all over the property. And today, I was harvesting.

Kneeling on the ground, I held the knife in one hand while I took the vine in the other. The chartreuse-colored vine was covered with a fuzz that felt a little sharp. I closed my eyes, still trying to shake away the weird vision the crows had brought, and concentrated.

"May Mother Earth bless my hands.
May the Green Man bless my deed.
Sweet pumpkin spirit, thank you for your gift.
Round and pregnant as the moon, I honor you.
May your flesh nourish.
May your seeds bring new life.
Thank you for your bounty.
In praise, I thank thee," I prayed then snipped the vine.

The little pumpkin's skin was a rich, dark orange color. I remembered then how my mom would always buy pie pumpkins at the grocery store around Thanksgiving. They were denser and darker than jack-o-lantern pumpkins. Halloween pumpkins were bright and light in comparison.

The thought of Halloween distracted me, calling Logan to mind. Since we started school in August, he always seemed nearby, close to me, but never close enough to have a proper conversation. I hoped Zoey was right, that he did like me, but if so, why was he keeping his distance? Maybe Nate had convinced him I was too weird. Maybe I was. The last thing I needed was a guy who didn't understand me.

I inhaled deeply, taking in the rich autumn scent and the smell of the gourds. I noticed that the old grape vines growing nearby were loaded this year. The pungent scent of grapes filled the air. The vines trailed down the mainly-broken trellis and across the ground to the south wall. The wall was covered with plum-colored grapes. Beyond the wall and the sloping hill, across a wide corn field, I spotted the Sanders barn. Their corn field, the shafts having turned a soft gold color, looked ready to be cut. I noticed then that they'd erected a scarecrow at the edge of the field. Its size and placement, however, looked odd. It wasn't tall enough or in the right place. But it must have worked. The crows were on my side of the fence, not theirs.

I stuck my knife back in my case, sliding it in where my blush brush should have gone.

"Only you would carry witch stuff rather than makeup," Mom had said the first time she'd seen it. "Can't you cast a spell so I can win the lottery or something?"

"How about I cast a spell that Larry moves out?"

"Amelia!"

"Well."

"Yeah. I know. But still, not even one tube of lipstick?"

"Hum. I have bee balm. Does that count?"

"I guess that's close enough," my mom had said then wandered off, shaking her head.

I smiled and stuck the makeup kit into my backpack then rose.

"Come on, bad girl," I told Bastet as I turned and headed back toward the house, pumpkin in hand.

When I got to the top of the rise, I paused and looked back toward the Sanders'. The scarecrow, I realized then, was gone. It hadn't been a straw man after all. Must have been Mister Sanders. What in the world had he been doing, checking the crop? I didn't know, but something felt wrong. Ugh. My energy was going haywire. I needed to get back to the house and drink some chamomile tea and dab myself with a couple of drops of lavender oil. Shaking off the odd feeling, I headed back to the house, black cat and pumpkin in tow.

CHAPTER FIVE

BASTET AND I SLIPPED BACK into the house just before the final breath of sunlight disappeared below the horizon. I slipped off my jacket and boots—Bastet disappearing on some new adventure—then headed toward the kitchen. The fastest way was through the narrow servant's corridor behind the grand staircase. On the east side of the house was the formal dining room. It was a massive space, large enough for thirty people to fit at the old oak table. The walls were covered in navy blue brocade wallpaper. The silver platters on the walls twinkled like stars when the lights were dim. The formal dining room was gorgeous, but a pain in the ass to clean. Last summer I had to take down all the platters and polish them. My back had ached for a week. Madame Knightly said her whole family used to dine there, but we never used the space. Instead, we always just kicked back in the ladies' parlor with a TV tray…just like Mom and I used to do at home before Larry—who always demanded a hot meal at the table—had messed up everything.

Madame Knightly was already waiting for me in the kitchen. She had a large pot of something bubbling on the stove.

"Ah! Will you look at that," she exclaimed happily, clasping her thin hands together when she saw the pumpkin.

"The field is covered with them."

"Really?" she asked in surprise. "Oh, I wish I could get out there to see it."

I smiled nicely at her, but the disturbing image the crows had evoked flashed through my mind. I shuddered. Hoping to exorcise the vision, I carried the pumpkin to the sink. I let the cold water wash over my hands, splashing some on my face. Then I started cleaning the pumpkin. "What's cooking?" I asked.

"I made the stock for a pumpkin soup. We'll roast what you have then add it in. I could barely remember the recipe. I hope it turns out right. My mother would make it every year when the pumpkins were ready."

Water flowed over the bumpy skin of the orange pumpkin, clearing away the grime from the field. I breathed deeply, inhaling the sharp scent of earth coming from the gourd, then set it aside.

Sticking my nose in Madame Knightly's pot, I smelled butter, milk, and a rich bouquet of herbs.

"Bring it here, Amelia," Madame Knightly said, motioning me toward the butcher table where a large knife was set out. It was a strange knife, not one of the regular kitchen utensils. I'd never seen it before, but right away I noticed its bone handle. The handle had been carved with unusual markings. I didn't recognize them.

"That's unusual," I said. Madame Knightly was, once more, either playing it coy or simply didn't know...that knife was a witch's tool.

"It's the pumpkin knife," she said with a laugh. "Mother kept it in the curio." She handed the knife to me. "Now, what did Mother always say?" Madame Knightly mused as she appeared to dig into the recesses of her memory. "Oh, yes, something like. 'Little pumpkin, count the days. Show me when the first frost's a'ways!' Now, cut it open."

I took the bone-handled knife from her. At once, I felt a jolt. The knife seemed to speak to me. It was pulsing with energy…not life, but magical energy. It was enchanted. I could hear its song, almost see its own memories. A voice—the knife's—filled my mind.

"How long?"

I slid the knife into the orange flesh, trimming out the stem.

"How long?"

How long for what? The frost? That didn't seem like the right question.

I set the cap aside, pulling out the long, sticky tendrils of the pumpkin's seedy innards. The sharp scent of the gourd filled the kitchen.

"There, now that smells like autumn," Madame Knightly said as she started picking the seeds off the cap's silky webbing. "Slice chunks to bake and put them in there," she directed me, pointing to a baking pan. "And put the seeds in there," she added, pointing to a cast iron frying pan sitting on the stove. "But not the nine of you," she said then, taking the small handful of seeds she'd collected.

I watched while Madame Knightly set the nine pumpkin seeds on the window sill.

Setting the enchanted knife down, I joined her.

"If the first frost will come within the next nine days, now we'll know it," she said, nodding at the seeds. "In the morning, the seeds will show us how many days are left."

"How?"

"You'll see."

I raised an eyebrow at her. Nine was a sacred number. It was the number of the Mother Goddess and a magical number. Madame Knightly, whether she knew it or not, was performing hearth magic. Maybe her mother had been a kitchen witch. Maybe the Knightlys had once been a magical family, but the knowledge had gotten lost down the generations. Or, maybe Madame Knightly was lying.

"Why nine?" I goaded.

Madame Knightly smiled wistfully out the window. "Mother always used nine," she said with a shrug, but this time, I saw a mischievous twinkle in her eye. It wasn't the first time I'd seen that look. "Let me help," she said then turned and stuck her hand into the pumpkin. She laughed. "I feel like a kid again."

I looked at the seeds set along the sill. *How long?* The question rung through my mind. Shaking off the thought, I turned and helped Madame Knightly prepare the pumpkin. While the large pieces were baking in the oven, Madame Knightly set me to the task of toasting the leftover seeds while she wandered off with the pumpkin knife, which she had cleaned and safely stowed back inside a long, wooden box.

Once the seeds were ready, I got started with my usual Friday night work: taking an inventory of the kitchen. I always prepared a grocery list that I'd call into the store the next morning. The store delivered Madame Knightly's food directly to the house. I was surprised, however, to discover that her kitchen was already stocked. Her pantry was bursting with canned food and other supplies, the fridge full of food. Madame Knightly was like that, still trying to take care of herself from time to time. Once I'd found her vacuuming the parlor. She looked so out of place with the old 50s vacuum. While her family's heyday was done, Madame Knightly still held a certain air about herself. Maybe it had something to do with her elevated, classy accent. Her tone wasn't quite Irish, though it had a small lilt to it. It was just refined, like her. She was a true lady, and she had no business with a vacuum.

I wandered off to work on the laundry instead. When that was done, the pumpkin had roasted long enough. I added it to the stock. Stirring slowly with a long-handled wooden spoon, I tossed in more herbs and splashed in some more heavy cream. The smell was divine. I let the soup cook down then pureed it with a handheld blender. Soon, the whole kitchen was filled with the delicious scents of roasted pumpkin, butter, cream, rosemary, cinnamon, and just a dash of cumin. I whipped together a quick pan of cornbread, and in no time, the meal was ready.

I prepared two trays and headed back to the ladies' parlor from which I could hear Madame Knightly's small TV. The TV, which had a slight green tint, looked as old as the vacuum. But it did the job. We always watched the evening news and a few of her favorite shows—including *Matlock*—before calling it a night.

"Oh, will you just smell that," she exclaimed when I entered with the trays. Madame Knightly had already set out our TV trays so we could watch and eat, as was our custom. "Thank you, my dear," she said as I placed the tray in front of her.

"And lots of toasted seeds for later."

Madame Knightly laughed happily then pointed at the TV as I settled in. "Have you seen this?" she asked. "There is rioting in LA."

"Really?"

"People are looting pharmacies. There was a shootout at a hospital."

Mom. A sudden terror swept over me as I read the scrawling banner. Hospitals around the United States were filling beyond capacity as flu cases swelled to epidemic proportions. A map of the U.S. suddenly appeared on the screen, showing the hardest hit places and where the flu was growing. As the map swelled red, I could see the virus was headed toward us.

"We'll be last," Madame Knightly said as she watched the screen. "Why don't you stay here with me? I spent all week watching cooking shows and went on a spending spree. I'm all stocked up. Surely they'll cancel school next week. Your mother will be run off her feet at the hospital. Maybe you'd better just stay here."

I stared at the scene on the TV, watching the map bloom again and again with red. A shiver ran down my back.

A moment later, Madame Knightly switched the channel to a rerun of *The Golden Girls*, forcing the bloody image away from my eyes.

"Amelia?"

"I'll have to check with Mom. I'm sure it would be okay," I said. Madame Knightly must have been scared. I didn't blame her. If I got sick, who would look after her? And the scenes on the TV were just...it was getting really bad. I hadn't seen anything like that before, not in the United States. "It will be okay," I muttered absently while Betty White cracked a joke about a goat.

"Yes, it will," Madame Knightly said then, setting her hand on mine.

When I turned to look at her, I saw she had a very serious look on her face.

Yep, she was definitely worried. I'd call Mom first thing in the morning.

"Now, let's have some of this beautiful soup," Madame Knightly said then turned her attention away, giggling at the TV while she blew on her spoon.

I stared down at the bowl, watching the steam lift in a strange, chaotic swirl, growing and rolling like the bloody map.

CHAPTER SIX

MADAME KNIGHTLY FELL ASLEEP IN front of the TV shortly after dinner. I woke the sweet old thing, who woke up muttering something about Witch Wood's gate, and led her to a small, private study just down the hallway from the library. Years earlier someone had moved Madame Knightly's bed there. She'd also moved most of her knickknacks, music boxes, jewelry chest, and clothes into the space. As I helped her shift into her night dress, I noticed the pumpkin knife box sitting on her bureau.

"Good night," I told her, lowering her into the bed.

"Good girl," she whispered. "So glad I have my good girl."

I smiled. "I'm glad I have you too." I could feel my heart cracking. How in the world was I going to leave her next fall and run off to college? Something just felt wrong about it, like maybe that wasn't what I was supposed to be doing. I needed to look again at online colleges. Maybe, if Madame Knightly got Internet service at Witch Wood, I could kill two birds with one stone. But even that didn't feel right.

I stopped to double-check that the front door was locked, I then headed back to the ladies' parlor and pulled out the blanket and pillow I had stashed in an ottoman out and flopped down on the chaise. School was going to get cancelled next week, that was a sure thing now…and just when I started making progress with Logan.

I sighed then pulled out my cell phone. Dead spot. No service, as usual. I snuggled down onto the chaise and pulled the blanket up to my neck. One of these days I was going to sleep upstairs in one of the massive bedrooms with their poster canopy beds. One of these days, but not tonight. I shivered. It was turning cold. Madame Knightly needed to show me how to turn on the heat. I didn't even know where the thermostat for the propane system was located.

Just as I closed my eyes, Bastet hopped onto the chaise. She stepped all over me, pausing to rub her head under my chin, then found an awkward spot near my head where she settled in for the night. I chuckled and fell off to sleep wearing a cat hat.

THE SOUND OF THE OLD rotary phone jangling startled me awake. I looked out the window to see that the sun had just barely risen. Everywhere was covered in mist.

The phone jangled loudly again. I sat up. Bastet was already gone. I hurried toward the phone in the kitchen. The wood floor was incredibly cold. I shivered, pulling my blanket around me. I lifted the old heavy old black receiver just as it chimed for the fifth time.

"Witch Wood Estate. This is Amelia. How may I help you?" I

said, speaking the greeting just as Madame Knightly had taught me.

"Amelia?" Mom's voice came through with a crackle.

"Mom? Is that you?"

"I can barely hear you. Can you hear me?" her voice sounded far away, like she was talking into a tin can. The line was full of static.

"Just. You okay?"

"I caught the flu. I've been puking since midnight, so they sent me home. But something weird happened. Larry is gone. The TV is still on, but he's nowhere…no phone calls, no nothing. The house was unlocked. Do you know where he is? Did he say anything to you?"

"No," I replied in surprise. Larry never went far from home. He might accidently get a job. "He was going to help Mrs. Sommers last night. She came over 'cause her furnace went out."

"Yeah, he was over there when I left. Oh, my God, I feel like I'm going to drop dead," my mom said then paused. I could just make out that she was rummaging around for something. "And I'm out of cigarettes. Great. If you hear from him, will you call me?"

"Mom, you shouldn't be smoking if you're sick. Do you have medicine? Maybe I should come home. I can stop by the Sommers' and see if they know where he went. You need to go to bed."

"No, hun. Stay out there. I don't want you getting this," she said and as if to accentuate the point, a moment later I could hear her puking in the background. She must have set down the phone. It sounded even hollower now.

"Mom?" I called. "Mom!"

After a minute, she picked up the phone again, but I could barely hear her. "Stay out there, baby girl. You'll be safer at Witch

Wood. I'll call you when I'm feeling better. Love you," she said, then the receiver went dead.

"Mom?"

I stared at the phone for a moment then hung it up. On the news they said people were dying in record numbers from the flu. Mom was right, I would be safer if I just stayed out here. But with Larry MIA, who would take care of her? Not that he was much use, but at least he could make her some soup or put her in bed. Where in the hell was he? Larry never left the house. I needed to go home. Vegetarians never got sick, right? I'd be fine.

I set the tea kettle on the burner. As I waited for it to boil, I looked outside. The fog was thick. I couldn't even make out the outline of the greenhouse that sat directly adjacent to the kitchen window. I turned to prepare the rest of the breakfast when the little pumpkin seeds sitting on the window sill caught my attention. The first little seed on the line was dry and golden in color. The rest, however, had turned moldy green and black. Hearth magic for certain. The seeds told a tale. There was no other way to explain the sudden decay of all of them except one. Magic ran strong in the Knightly family, whether they knew it or not. But what, exactly, did it mean? Would it frost today? Tonight? I frowned. Seems as if the answer to the question, *how long*, was simply one night.

As I prepared Madame Knightly's breakfast, I warred with myself. I loved Mom, and she didn't have anyone but me. Madame Knightly also didn't have anyone but me. I needed to do something. I just couldn't leave my mom in a condition like that. By the time the tea, toast, boiled egg, and blackberries were ready, I'd made up my mind.

I carried the tray as quietly as possible to Madame Knightly's room just in case she was still asleep. As usual, however, she was awake and lying in bed reading. She was looking at the book written in Latin I'd recovered the day before.

"I didn't know you could read Latin," I told her as I set her breakfast tray on the side table.

"Latin, Greek, French, Turkish, and even a dialect of old Celtic," she said with a smile.

"Who taught you?"

"Well, when I was a girl, I had a very bright tutor, and I've got a quick mind for languages," she said then set down the book. "Did I hear the phone?"

"Yes," I said as I pulled the breakfast tray beside her bed. "My mom got the flu. She's really sick, and my stepdad is missing. I was thinking—"

"You want to go check on her," Madame Knightly said kindly.

"If you could spare me for just a couple of hours? I just need to see where Larry went. He'll look after Mom…in his way. I'll grab the rest of my things and come back to stay, like we talked about."

When I looked back at her again, I saw Madame Knightly was gazing out the window. The sun had broken over the horizon, filling the sky with shades of pink and orange.

"What did your mother say for you to do?"

"To stay at Witch Wood, that I'll be safer here."

"She's right."

"I know, but I can't leave her like that. She's worried about him, and sick, and exhausted. Like they said on TV last night, people are dying from the flu."

Madame Knightly smiled. "All right then, Amelia. We'll see you back soon."

"Do you need me to pick up anything in town?"

Madame Knightly shook her head. "I have everything I need here."

"The phone reception was really terrible. I think the line is going."

Madame Knightly shook her head. "It's just the mist. It always…" Madame Knightly said, then paused as if searching for the right words. "It always disrupts the connection."

"Can I do anything else before I go? There's still leftover soup in the fridge. Do you need anything?"

"No. Just be careful."

I hugged her tightly, feeling her frail frame in my arms. "Madame Knightly, maybe I shouldn't…"

"Go and hurry back, my dear. Remember, you are always welcome and safe at Witch Wood."

"Thank you. Thank you so much."

Madame Knightly nodded then inclined her head to me.

"I'll be quick. I promise."

She nodded but said nothing more, simply reaching over for her teacup.

Feeling guilty, I headed back to the front of the house and picked up my backpack, the key, and pulled on my coat. The old front door was sticky. The fog must have expanded the wood. It took me all my strength to pull the door open. Outside, it was still foggy. I pulled out my cell phone. Still no reception. Sighing, I grabbed my bike.

A moment later, I felt a brush against my shins. Bastet.

"I'm glad the mice haven't found your secret passageway in and out of the place yet," I told her. She meowed at me then rubbed her head against my leg.

With Bastet trotting along beside me, I headed down the lane in the dense fog, walking my bike as I went. You could barely see three feet in front of you. In the mist, the gate came up on me suddenly. I stopped and pushed it open, guiding my bike to the other side. Knowing her place, Bastet stayed inside the gate.

"See you soon," I told the little black cat who merely meowed in reply then flicked her tail back and forth like she was annoyed at me for leaving.

I was surprised to find that along the road, the mist had completely cleared. When I looked back at Witch Wood, however, the place was completely lost in the fog. Not even the chimneys shown above the mist. Odd.

I hopped on my bike and peddled back toward town. As I rode off, I checked my small round rearview mirror. I spotted a figure on the road behind me. Mister Sanders. Was he headed to the bluff? I biked past the walking path that led to the spot, a steep cliff with a large pond at the base. Kids used to swim there until someone jumped off the bluff's edge into the pond and broke his neck. That happened when my mom was a kid. She'd been friends with the boy.

I glanced back at Mister Sanders once more. He was walking so unhurriedly. I guess he, just like Madame Knightly, was slowing down too. Guilt stole over me again, but I reminded myself that Mom needed me. I turned my attention ahead and peddled fast toward home.

CHAPTER
SEVEN

AS I RODE BACK INTO town, the scene that unfolded confused me. Several people were outside their houses nailing wood planks and plastic over the windows. I saw people unloading cases of food into their home. Even more, I saw families packing up their cars, the trunks full of supplies. Many people were wearing surgical masks. Several vehicles whipped past me, and in the distance, I could hear the wail of sirens.

There was a line of cars parked all the way down Nineteenth Avenue. It wasn't until I passed the gas station that I saw people had been lined up for more than a mile to get gas. The scene was the same but much more chaotic at the bank. The bank's doors were closed…but it was Saturday morning. People stood outside banging on the glass.

"Open the damned door," I heard a man roar.

The voices grew louder, and as I biked away, I heard the crashing sound of glass.

I didn't even look back, just peddled harder. As I turned the corner at Fifth Avenue, however, I nearly ran into a guy wearing a gas mask pushing a completely loaded grocery cart. I swerved to miss him and had to jump off my bike to keep from falling.

"Sorry, Amelia," he said, stopping for just a moment to help me pick up the bike.

My heart pounding in my chest, I looked at the guy once again. I realized then that it was Brian.

"Brian? What in the hell is going on?" I asked.

"Don't go to the grocery store. It's scary in there. People are starting to freak. You better go straight home," he said through the mask. "I'd take you to make sure you get there okay, but Brianna and Mom are at home...I don't want to leave them for long. My dad was sick, and on the TV they said..." but his voice trailed off.

"It's okay," I told him. "I'm headed there now. Be safe."

"You too," he told me then headed off once more.

I looked down the street toward the grocery store. I could see red and blue police lights flickering. Mom never kept anything to eat at home. I hoped she had enough to get her through. If not, once she was feeling better, I could take her to Witch Wood. A guilty feeling swept over me. If people were starting to lose it, Madame Knightly wasn't safe alone out there. I needed to go back. If people started looting, they might go to the old estate looking for valuables.

My thoughts were interrupted by the peppering sound of gunfire coming from the grocery store followed by the sound of a police officer's voice over a PA system.

I turned my bike and pushed fast toward home.

Larry's old truck and Mom's bug were parked in the driveway. I cast a glance across the street and saw that the front door to the Sommers' two-story house was hanging wide open. I leaned my bike against the tree, setting my hand on the trunk for just a moment in greeting.

I jotted up the steps, pulling my keys out of my pocket, only to find the door was ajar. I could feel the heat inside the house wafting through the small crack. I pushed the door open and went inside, dropping my pack at the door. I closed and locked the door behind me.

"Mom?" I called.

The TV was on, but there was no one in the living room. The TV was broadcasting the same kind of images I'd seen with Madame Knightly the night before. This morning it showed the image of a riot in Philadelphia. The scrawling banner underneath dictated which states, not cities, were now under martial law. Connecticut was now on the list. A moment later the TV switched from national to local news. A familiar looking TV reporter came on.

"Good morning. The situation in the country this morning is grim..."

"Mom? Larry?"

I headed down the hallway toward the back of the house. It was quiet. I couldn't hear Larry snoring. I looked into my room. It was exactly as I'd left it the day before. The bathroom door was hanging open. I could see Mom had been there. Her dirty scrubs were lying on the floor and a can of ginger ale sat on the bathroom counter.

"Mom?" I whispered, thinking she was probably sleeping, then pushed the door to her bedroom open only to find the room was completely empty. The bed was unmade, but no one was there. Was she out looking for Larry? Had she gone out for something…for cigarettes?

I headed back to the living room.

"Residents are advised to stay inside their homes. A second concern for our area is the increasing number of people fleeing New York City to the countryside for shelter, many of which are armed. Use extreme caution. Do not leave your homes unless you must. Call emergency hotlines only where there is extreme need. Local hospitals are flooded. The CDC has issued reports that the infected are suffering unusual side effects and can be dangerous. There have been reports of the inflicted attacking—"

I muted the TV and pulled out my cell phone. I had messages from Zoey, but I slid my finger past them and dialed Mom's number. I was surprised when I heard her ringtone, the *Harry Potter* theme song, chime from the kitchen. I rose to discover her purse was slung over the corner of a kitchen chair. Her car keys were still in the candy dish turned catch-all on the table.

I thumbed through Zoey's messages asking where I was, if I was at Witch Wood, that her work was cancelled because the coffee shop was closed, and finally that her little sister had gone missing. I dialed her number. After a moment, the line picked up but she didn't say hello.

"Zoey?" I called.

No answer.

"Zo? Can you hear me?"

I pressed my ear against the phone. I could hear Zoey. She was talking. But I couldn't hear what she was saying. "Zoey," I yelled into the phone.

A moment later, the line went dead.

I sent her a text. *Tried to call. Line was funny. I'm back in town. Mom and Larry are MIA. Where are you? WTF is going on?*

I looked out across the street toward the Sommers'. No doubt Mom had gone looking for Larry.

Heading back outside, I walked toward the Sommers' house. As I crossed the lawn, however, the large old oak shifted in the breeze, casting an avalanche of orange-colored leaves down on me. I stopped a moment and noticed the tree's aura looked brighter, more red. It swayed in the breeze, the leaves and acorns dropping all around me. It was then, however, that I noticed that it wasn't windy at all. All the same, the tree was moving.

I cast a glance back at the Sommers' house, at the open door, and I squinted my eyes to really see, to see what only I could see. And I could see that the Sommers house was surrounded by a dark aura. Swirling red and black light whirled all around the front door.

I gasped.

The tree stilled.

I turned and headed back inside, stopping once more to set my hand on my beloved oak.

"Thank you," I whispered then headed into the house, closing and locking the door behind me.

CHAPTER
EIGHT

HANDS SHAKING, I PULLED OUT my phone again. Nothing from Zoey.

Feeling like a snoop, I grabbed my mom's bag and pulled out her cell phone. She had several missed calls from work. Her best friend Emma had texted twice asking if she was feeling better. Mom hadn't answered.

Uncertain what to do next, I dialed 911. For love of the Goddess, my mother was sick, and she was missing.

The line rang, and rang, and rang, and rang. After nearly five minutes of waiting, I hung up. No answer on 911? I stared at the TV. The scenes were bloody and violent. They were airing someone's cell phone footage. The person was running, their cell recording. A moment later, they got jumped. The TV paused on the face of the attacker. He was a male with a large gash down the side of his face. His mouth dripped with bloody saliva. When the film went live again, you could see the camera tumble from the victim's hands then showed a glimpse of the man biting into the victim's flesh.

Grabbing the remote, I turned the volume back up. The TV broke back to the female reporter. The male reporter who was usually at her side was missing.

"Reports of these kinds of attacks, and seemingly rabid behavior, are coming in from all over the United States. The illness is putting the infected into a schizoid state wherein they…they are turning on their loved ones. They are biting, and in some reports, eating, the living, a delusional form of cannibalism.

"Stay inside your homes. Emergency services are stretched to their limits as the number of infected is growing exponentially."

Sick to my stomach, I turned off the TV.

I headed back to my bedroom and opened up my box of shadows. Inside were my magical items. I pulled on a protective amulet I had made for myself out of shells, stones, and rowan wood. I grabbed my notebook filled with spells I had written, my crystals, and my pouch full of dried herbs. Last summer Zoey and I had gone to a Renaissance Faire where I'd purchased a small headband made of silver with the waxing and waning moon symbols thereon. I put it on.

"Great Mother, protect me. Father God, protect me," I whispered.

A moment later, I heard a thump from the other room.

"Mom?"

There was no answer.

Moving slowly, I went back to the living room. The front door was still closed. I looked out the window. The vehicles were still in the driveway, and the Sommers' door was still open.

I slid my magical items into my backpack and put it on.

I didn't know how, exactly, but I knew I was in danger. I needed to get out of here. Moving quickly, I flipped over an envelope lying on the table and scrawled a note for my mom to call me at Witch Wood as soon as she got home. While I didn't know where she was, I could feel I wasn't safe. I had to go back to Witch Wood.

Thump. Again, the noise. It sounded like a bird had flown into the sliding glass door that led to the backyard. It happened on occasion. But it wasn't a bird. While the window drapes had been pulled shut, I could see the silhouette of someone standing at the door outside.

Thump. The person banged against the door only to stand there thereafter, not moving, not knocking, just standing there.

I gasped and looked around, then grabbed a large knife from the knife block.

There was only one way in and out of our fenced backyard… through the glass door. I stared at the shadow, distorted by the waves in the fabric.

"Mom?" I whispered.

The person thumped against the door again. Mom kept a pack of cigarettes hidden in the tool shed. Had she gone outside to get them? But if it was her, why wasn't she answering? Mustering up my courage, the knife poised at the ready, I reached forward with a shaking hand and snatched the curtain back.

Mom stood on the other side of the door. It was her, but she looked…wrong. Her skin was deathly pale. Her eyes had gone moon white. Her mouth hung open. She hissed and slammed against the door, smearing bloody saliva across the glass.

I stepped backward, the knife dropping from my hand.

"Mom?"

Out of the corner of my eye I spotted something lying in the backyard. At first it looked like a pile of laundry, but a moment later I identified the purple pansy print fabric of the dress Mrs. Sommers had been wearing the day before. Her body lay slumped in the backyard. Her dress was stained with blood.

Mom slammed against the door again. Her mouth, hands, and chest were caked in blood. She was wearing a white tank top, and her mint-colored scrub bottoms. Both were stained red. Blood and a piece of something pink and pulpy were stuck to her name necklace. The delicate gold of her name, Caroline, was stained red.

"Mom!"

She hissed and slammed at the door once more.

I focused hard, looking at the energy around her. It was completely…infected. The sticky blackness I had seen the day before snaked around her energy. The glimmering colors that always surrounded her life force had been completely replaced by it.

"Mom," I whimpered, reaching out to touch the glass.

Seeing my hand, my mother snapped at it, tiling her head weirdly as she looked at it and me.

My heart cracked in half and tears rolled down my cheeks. I was too late to help her. Whatever was happening to the others had happened to her too. My mom…she wasn't right. What had she done to Mrs. Sommers? I couldn't believe my eyes.

I pulled out the phone and dialed 911 again. Again there was no answer.

"Mom, can you hear me?"

Again, she snapped at me. I remember what the reporter had said, that the infected were dangerous. My mom…was dangerous.

How could it be? Hot tears trailed down my cheeks. What could I do? What could I do to help her? I reached out and touched the glass, stroking it along her cheek.

"I love you," I whispered, shuddering as I cried.

My mother slammed herself against the glass again, this time hitting the glass so hard I thought it might break. I gasped.

At the front of the house, I heard an engine. I looked outside to see Zoey's old van.

I backed away from the terrible image toward the front door. Pulling it open, I rushed outside and down the steps.

"Amelia," Zoey screamed from the open van window.

In that same moment, the oak tree shifted wildly, and I turned to see Larry crash through the fire bushes at the side of the yard. He was in the same condition as Mom, blood dripping down his shirt. That same black aura surrounded him. He rushed toward me.

"Amelia! No," Zoey yelled then jumped out of the van.

Larry was nearly on me in a heartbeat.

"No! Get back," I shouted, envisioning—and feeling—a bolt of white light shooting from my hands toward him.

Larry grunted and fell backward.

Gasping, I stared at him.

"What did you do?" Zoey exclaimed, looking from me to Larry who was getting up again.

"I…I'm not sure."

"Let's go," Zoey said then, pulling me toward her van. We jumped in and slammed the doors shut. Larry rushed to the back of the van and grabbed the rear windshield wiper.

Zoey gunned it, and Larry fell, blood smearing the glass.

"Jesus Christ," Zoey swore.

"Pretty sure he has nothing to do with this," I muttered. I stared down at my hands. What had I done? What...how had I done that?

"Unless he's, like, planning to show up later today or something. Where's your mom?"

"Messed up. Sick. She's in the backyard. She got sick... she...what am I supposed to do? I can't just leave her there. I keep calling 911," I said then pulled out my phone and dialed it again. Again, no answer. "Where's your sister?"

Zoey shook her head. "Like Larry and Caroline. My parents hightailed it out of here last night for their hunting camp. They left without us, told me to come when she showed up. They thought she was just out running with boys all night. They were so pissed at her. She turned up this morning all messed up and then she...she had some weird convulsion and after that she wasn't right. I...I locked her in the house and took off. I was about to go to Witch Wood when I got your text.

I shook my head, tears streaming down my face. "What do we do? They're sick. What do we do?"

"I...I don't know. But I saw some crazy shit driving over here. I think it's here. It's bad here now. We need to get somewhere safe."

"Witch Wood. We'll be safe out there, and I can't leave Madame Knightly alone."

"What about B. and B.?" Zoey asked. It was the nickname we called Brianna and Brian.

"I passed Bri on my way into town. He was headed home with groceries."

Zoey nodded. "We'll stop by their house." She turned her van that direction. When we got to the intersection, an unusual sight caught both of our attention. "Do you see that?" she asked.

Down the street, I saw the grocery store was now on fire, and there was a fight taking place in the parking lot. I heard gunshots.

"Christ," Zoey swore again, turning away from the scene and driving up a backstreet.

"Can you shoot?" Zoey asked, shoving a handgun at me.

"No," I said, waving it away. "Where did you get that?"

"Me either. It can't be hard, right? I loaded it, but never shot it before. My freaking dad. He left the gun with me and ran off. So much for that protective parental instinct."

"That's screwed up."

"Well, they're assholes. They only think of themselves."

Zoey pulled the van into the driveway of Brian's and Brianna's small house.

The shopping cart Brian had been pushing was lying in the yard toppled over. Canned food and bottled water was spilled across the lawn. The front door was open.

"Not good," Zoey said, echoing my own thoughts.

We sat for a moment and thought what to do. A second later, however, we heard commotion and Brianna and Brian—Brian still wearing the gas mask—came running out the house, their dad fast on their heels. Blood was streaked down the front of his shirt.

"Oh, my God," Zoey said then jumped out of the van.

Hands shaking, I followed.

"Get in," Zoey yelled to them then grabbed the shovel that was leaning against the mailbox.

Brianna tore across the yard toward us. She was still wearing her pajamas and didn't have any shoes on. She got to the van first.

"Bri, come on," she yelled back to her brother.

Brian rushed, but his dad reached for him, grabbing him by the back of the shirt. Brian tried to pull himself loose but couldn't get free. Zoey swept in and nailed their dad hard on the back with the shovel. He let go.

"Brian," Brianna screamed.

I backed toward the van, sliding back into the seat, as their dad turned and lunged at Zoey.

"Dad, no," Brian yelled.

Zoey heaved the shovel back and hit the man hard against the side of the head.

He fell.

"Get in," I called to them.

Brian stood staring at his father who lay twitching on the ground.

"What's happening?" Brianna cried. "What's wrong with him? Bri, come on!"

At the sound of his sister's voice, Brian turned and rushed to the van.

Throwing the shovel down, Zoey jumped into the van. She put the van into reverse just as Brian and Brianna's dad began to rise slowly from the ground.

"He's getting up," I whispered. I looked hard and around him I saw that same black, contaminated aura.

"Zoey, go, go, go," Brian cried.

Zoey whipped the van back and headed off.

"What the hell!" Brian said. "What the actual hell!"

"Dad was…he was eating Mom!" Brianna said with a shudder.

Brian wrapped is arm around his sister.

"It's like it happened overnight," Zoey said.

I shook my head. "It's been happening. On the news....it's been happening in other places. I don't think anyone understood what was going on, not really. Mom...she said people have been really sick at the hospital. It's been building."

"Where's your mom?" Brianna asked.

"In our backyard. She's like your dad."

Brian pulled off his gasmask. "Zoey, head over to the school."

"What for?"

"Nate, Logan, and some others are over there. They're in trouble."

"And why should I care? We're going to Witch Wood. Screw them."

"Zoey," Brian exclaimed.

"Nate's a dick. I don't care what happens to him," she replied.

"Yeah, me either. But the people who are with him aren't."

Zoey sighed heavily.

"Amelia, come on," Brian said.

Zoey looked at me with a questioning expression on her face.

"Logan," I said. My heart hurt at the idea that he was in trouble. If I could help him, I would.

"Fine," Zoey said tartly and turned the car in the direction of the high school.

CHAPTER
NINE

ZOEY TURNED TOWARD THE HIGH school. All the houses along the street were boarded up. Nothing moved. We pulled into the school parking lot. It was nearly empty. The looming building was dark. Brian was texting furiously.

"No one's answering. They were hiding out in the nurse's office. Katie's sister freaking bit her. She panicked and called Jenna who called Nate. He and the others brought Katie here since there was a riot at the Medical Center in town. Dammit, they aren't responding."

Lifting my cell, I tried 911 again. Again, the line was busy.

"Let's just go. Who the hell knows where they are," Zoey said.

Brianna had been weeping softly the whole time. Her words rang through my head. Her dad had eaten her mom. Eaten. Was that what my mom had been doing to Mrs. Sommers? Eating her? I inhaled deeply and tried not to cry. No. No way. She couldn't do something like that. She was just sick. I just needed to get back to Witch Wood and figure out a way to help her.

"I don't even have any shoes on," Brianna sobbed. "No phone, no purse, no shoes. Nothing. Bri, Dad got up. Did you see that? He got up?"

"I saw," Brian replied, his forehead furrowing.

"What does it mean? Zoey hit him hard enough to knock him out. But he got up. What does it mean?"

"I don't know," Brian answered somberly.

"Amelia? Do you...do you know anything?" Brianna asked. "You know, the way you know stuff sometimes."

Everyone turned and looked at me.

"They're infected. It's like something is eating up the goodness—the light—inside them."

Zoey stared at me with her big blue eyes. I could read the question thereon: *And what about the other thing that happened?*

"I don't know, Zo," I whispered, answering her unvoiced question.

She nodded but didn't ask me anything else. Instead, she reached across and took my hand, squeezing it reassuringly. It felt so comforting to feel her energy close to mine. I exhaled deeply.

A moment later, my cell buzzed. I looked down to see a message from Logan. How had he gotten my number? *We are in the cafeteria but trapped. I can see you. Come to service entrance?*

"Logan," I said then relayed his message.

Zoey drove her van across the parking lot toward the back of the school where the loading platform and dumpster were nestled in the narrow alley. Moving slowly, we all got out and headed up the back stairs.

I sent Logan a text. *Here.*

We waited a few minutes, but there was no reply.

"He's not answering."

"Bri, they're right. Let's go. If Amelia can take us to Witch Wood—" Brianna began, but Brian waved his hand to cut her off.

"Shush," Brian said, straining to listen. "I hear something."

Zoey pulled out the handgun. She nodded to Brian who grabbed for the door, but it was locked.

"We'll try the front," Brian whispered.

"They said they were trapped. There must be someone sick inside," Zoey protested.

"Well, we can't just leave them in there," Brian retorted.

I frowned then texted Logan again. *We're here. Where are you?*

From inside we heard a terrible clatter followed by the sound of a girl screaming.

"Was that Jenna?" Brianna whispered, aghast.

"Let's go," Brian said then we headed to the front door. There, we found the corner door, which the janitor always left open on the weekends while he was working, open just a crack.

We entered quietly. The main entrance of the school had a large, open foyer where couches and chairs dating back to at least the seventies were placed along with dusty potted plants and silk trees. The white tile floor was glaringly clean. All the lights were off. The place was exceedingly quiet. Trailing away from the foyer were two long hallways. They were empty. The main office on the other side of the building was dark, the door closed.

"This way," Brian said. "Let's go to the cafeteria."

"You mean go toward the scream?" Zoey whispered. "That's how people in horror movies die."

"We aren't in a horror movie. And our friends are in trouble."

"Your friends," Zoey grumbled under her breath.

"My locker is just there," Brianna whispered, pointing. "I have shoes inside. Please, can we stop real quick?"

Brian nodded, and we headed down the hallway following behind him.

"Did you see their dad?" Zoey whispered to me. "I hammered him hard…like deep backfield hard," Zoey said. "He got up like nothing was wrong."

"On TV they said the virus was making people go crazy, turning them into schizoid cannibals. My mom…Mrs. Sommers' body was lying in our backyard. It was bloody. Mom had blood on her."

"What the hell kind of virus is this?" Zoey said, shaking her head.

"I don't know." But I did know. I could see how it was changing people's very life force. Their energy was disrupted, polluted.

Down the hallway from us, Brianna opened her locker quietly, gently pulling up the metal lock. Noiselessly, she slipped on her gym shoes and a coat.

I paused as we passed the nurse's office. Inside, I saw heaps of bandages and blood on the floor. The desk chair was flipped over, and all the items on the desk had been shoved to the floor.

From the other end of the building, we heard a crash and another scream.

"We need to get out of here," Zoey whispered.

I pulled out my phone again. It was almost out of battery, and there was no message.

"Not yet," Brian said. "Please, Zoe."

She sighed heavily, and we headed toward the cafeteria.

My hands shook. Something was bad here.

When we passed the athletic office, Brian motioned for us to stop. He opened the door slowly then slipped inside. A moment later, he came back carrying two baseball bats. He handed one to his sister.

"There were only two," he told me, frowning with regret.

"I'll be okay," I reassured him. I looked down at my hands. The aura around them was vibrant, glowing so bright that I was surprised the others couldn't see it. Magic lived in the world just parallel to us, operating on wavelengths unseen by most human beings, but felt by some of us. Those in tune with the otherworld felt magic, could conjure it, could change their world and lives just by getting on the right wavelength. If you felt the energy, you could harness it to do your will. Was that how my spell worked? Had I tapped into this force in a new way? My emotions were strong when Larry had appeared, but strong enough to make that energy materialize in this plane of existence in a corporeal way? Larry, who had never felt anything beyond the material realm, had been knocked off his feet by my spell. How? How had that happened?

When we finally reached the cafeteria, we peaked into the back window and saw a terrible sight. Katie was infected, that was for sure, and so was Brad, another of Nate's friends. They were clawing at the door of the utility closet. On the cafeteria floor lay what was left of Jenna. Her entire stomach had been ripped open, her arms and legs torn to pulpy, bloody shreds. She stared, vacant-eyed, across the cafeteria. Sam, her best friend, was busy gnawing her insides.

Brianna gasped, covering her mouth. Unable to control herself, she turned and vomited, the puke shooting through her fingers.

We slid out of sight.

"I don't know," Zoey told Brian. "There are three of them. I don't know if I can shoot this thing. We can't...I can't just shoot them."

"But the others must be inside," Brian said.

"We don't have to kill anyone," I said. "Let's just lure them out. Zoey, you and Brian are fast. Open the front doors then make a ton of noise, lure them out of there then use the alley to head back to the van. Brianna and I will get the others out of the closet as soon as they go off after you."

"Reasonable in an insane kind of way," Zoey said.

"You okay with that?" Brian asked his sister who was shaking and pale.

She nodded.

Brian looked at Zoey. "Come on."

I took Brianna gently by the arm, and we ducked into the ladies' restroom just down the hallway from the cafeteria. I held the door open just the tiniest crack.

Brianna turned the water on very gently and washed her face and mouth.

We waited, and a moment later, we heard noise coming from the front of the school. I hoped it was enough to lure the others out without getting the attention of anyone else who happened to be lingering around.

Brianna turned off the water then stood beside me, waiting.

A moment later, we heard footsteps rushing down the hallway.

First Brad, then Katie and Sam, moved past. I could just make out their movements.

"*Goddess, Mother, don't let them see us. The door is sealed. They hear nothing. Smell nothing. See nothing. We aren't here. The door is closed. They see only the closed door.*" I envisioned the ladies' room door fully closed, that from the hallway they could not see anything as they passed. I envisioned it perfectly, then held my breath. A moment later, through the window on the opposite wall, I saw that all three of them had exited the building. When they turned the corner out of sight, I nodded to Brianna and pushed the door open.

We raced quickly into the cafeteria, skirting around the massive pool of blood and heap of bloody remains that Jenna had become.

"Oh, Jenna," Brianna whispered.

"Don't look at it," I told her.

I hurried to the door then knocked gently. "Logan? Are you in there?"

"Amelia?" Logan replied.

"It's clear."

I stepped back.

The door opened and Logan, Nate, and Nate's older sister, Madison, who I thought was away at college, emerged.

Madison gasped when she saw what was left of Jenna.

"Hurry," I said then led them across the cafeteria. Outside, I heard tires squeal.

We raced down the hall, moving fast. When we turned the corner, however, we found Mister Anderson, the janitor, standing between us and the door. His eyes were milky white, bloody saliva dripping from his chin.

Madison shrieked and ducked behind her brother.

Mister Anderson lunged at Logan who dodged. Brianna took the opportunity to dart around us and head out the door, Nate and Madison following behind her. I scanned around for anything to use as a weapon, but there was nothing.

The van pulled up outside. I heard Zoey yell, "Come on!"

"Here," Logan said then, waving at Mister Anderson who had turned toward me. "No, over here," he called again as he backed toward the lobby chairs.

Mister Anderson followed after him, but Logan leapt over the chairs. He stopped and picked up one of the end tables.

"Amelia, run," he called to me.

I turned and headed toward the door. Looking over my shoulder, I saw Logan hurl the table at Mister Anderson. It hit him in the chest and he fell.

"Let's go," Logan said, and raced to the door.

"Go! Go! Let's go," Zoey screamed.

Brad, Katie, and Sam were closing in on the van.

Logan and I jumped into the van, sliding the door shut behind us as Zoey gassed it, turning the van in the direction of Witch Wood.

CHAPTER

TEN

"TAKE US TO THE COUNTRY club," Nate said as Zoey sped away from the high school.

"What?" Zoey retorted.

"The. Country. Club," Nate replied.

"I'm not deaf," Zoey told him. "And you're welcome very much," she added, turning the van in the direction of the country club.

"Yeah, whatever, thanks," Nate mumbled halfway under his breath.

"Where are you going?" Logan asked me.

"Witch Wood Estate. It's a place outside of town. I take care of someone out there. It's remote. Safe. You could come with us."

"Screw that," Nate said. "My dad called me from the club. He and Mom were there with a bunch of other people. They had guns and food and had locked the place up. Don't puss out, Logan. Come with me and Maddie."

"Did you see Jenna?" Madison was saying, staring out the window. "Did you see what they did to her? They ate her! They ate her!"

"They're sick," Brian said.

"Sick? What the hell kind of sick is that? That's not sick, that's crazy…like they lost their minds kind of crazy. Nate. Nate, we need to get to Mom and Dad. We're gonna get killed out here," Madison said, panic filling her voice.

"Calm down, Maddie. We're almost there," he told her.

Logan leaned forward and turned on the radio. There was a recorded message playing on every station. It listed the U.S. states under quarantine. Otherwise, nothing was playing.

Nate was texting furiously.

"Is Mom answering? Is Dad answering? Nate? What did Dad say to do?" Madison said, grabbing Nate's arm.

"Jesus, Maddie. I can't type when you do that. Nothing. Nothing, they aren't saying anything. Dad isn't answering."

"What about your family?" I asked Logan. "Your sister?"

"My sister and I…we're fosters. Our foster parents just disappeared. I called Addison's biological grandparents last night. They came and got her, said they'd take care of her. My foster mom and dad never came home."

"Maybe they're at the club," Nate told him. "Your dad is always there."

"Drunk," Logan muttered under his breath.

He then looked at me, those gold-colored eyes meeting mine again. "Witch Wood?"

"It will be safe there."

Logan nodded, but didn't say another word.

Zoey turned her van down the road leading to the country club. The fence was lying in the middle of the drive, completely smashed down.

"What is that?" Madison asked, leaning forward.

"It looks like someone knocked the fence in, drove over it," Zoey answered. "I don't know, man. This doesn't look good." Zoey then slowly maneuvered her van over the broken fence.

The parking lot of the swanky Brighton Country Club, just one of the many businesses in Brighton owned by Nate's dad, was full of cars: Lexus, Audi, Mercedes, BMW, and Cadillac. It was like a luxury car convention. The windows on the long building, which backed up to the golf course, were shuttered. Nothing moved outside.

"Look," Logan said, pointing.

The shutter on the front door had been pried open. Broken glass littered the entryway sidewalk.

"We need to get out of here," Brian said.

"Zoey, stop here," Nate said.

She put the van in park then turned and looked at me. She shook her head.

"Come on, Logan, Maddie," Nate said then reached over and opened the door.

Wordlessly, Madison followed her brother. Logan, however, didn't get out.

"Don't be a fag," Nate told him. "Let's go."

"I don't know. Maybe Amelia has the better idea. If your parents aren't answering…"

Pissed, Nate turned with his sister and headed toward the building.

"Okay, are we done with this now?" Zoey asked, looking back at Brian. "Shut the door," she told him then put the van into drive.

Zoey spun the van around the parking lot and headed back out when I set my hand on hers. It was wrong. I despised Nate, but it was wrong to leave them like that. Nate was stupid and an asshole, and Madison was freaking out, but we were leaving them to die. They just didn't know it.

"Zoe."

She slowed. "Dammit. Yeah, I know," she said then stopped and put the van into reverse.

"I hate Nate," Brian said. "God, I hate him so much right now," he said, and when the van stopped, he opened the door and grabbed his baseball bat.

We all got out of the van and walked carefully toward the club. From inside, we heard the sound of breaking glass.

"Bri?" Brianna whispered, her voice trembling.

"Stay close to me," he told her.

We entered the posh building. Overhead, a massive crystal chandelier swayed in the breeze. It was dim inside save the light offered by the skylight in the foyer. There, sunlight shone down on the large water fountain. The water was still. On closer inspection, I noticed it was tinged with blood.

Brian and Brianna held their baseball bats tight while Zoey gripped her revolver.

"Which way?" Zoey whispered when we came to the main hallway.

I stared down the passages. My instincts nagged at me, pulling me right.

"Right," I whispered then headed down the hall. I'd only been in the country club once for my mom's Christmas dinner for work. One of the doctors had taken all the nurses who worked on his floor out for a nice meal. We walked down the hallway toward the restaurant. The walls were made of heavy, highly polished oak. Photos of tournaments, soft-looking pennants, and oil paintings of fox hunts decorated the walls.

In the distance, we heard a door slam followed by a scream. A second later, someone appeared in the hallway in front of us. The person, an older woman with white hair, limped into the hall. One of her high heels was missing. She wandered into the corridor then stopped, looking in the direction of the noise.

Brianna started to back away but bumped against the wall, banging into the fire hydrant. The hydrant fell onto the floor with a thud.

The woman turned and looked at us.

She was infected. She moved toward us, limping in her one shoe.

"This way," Brian said then, pushing open a side door that led into the bar. We followed behind him. Once inside, he motioned to Logan and the two of them pushed a door in front of the table. The scene in the bar was a disaster. There were broken glasses and bottles lying all over the place. In the corner a body was slumped against the wall. Whoever he was, the man had been shot in the head.

"Nate," Logan whispered.

There was no answer, but after a moment, we heard noise from behind the bar.

Logan lifted a finger to his lips and crossed the room quickly, crawling up on a bar stool. He looked over.

"Miss Beatrice?"

A moment later, Miss Beatrice rose. She was gripping a large knife, her well-manicured hands squeezing the handle so hard her knuckles had turned white. There was a splatter of blood across her pretty face. Her long, blonde hair looked like it was matted with some sort of goo.

"Logan?" she said then looked at the rest of us. "What are you all doing here?"

"We came with Nate," Zoey answered. "We got…separated."

Miss Beatrice nodded. "Allen and I were with his mom and dad. We got separated too. I don't know what happened. We were locked in. Everything was okay and then it wasn't. I was waiting for Allen to come back. You see anyone?"

Not living. "A woman. Out there. She's not well," I said. And then, as if on cue, someone pushed on the door.

"What happened there?" Zoey asked, pointing to the man in the corner.

"He got sick, tried to jump someone. The bartender shot him," she replied as she slowly came around the bar.

"Let's find the others and get out of here," Logan said.

Miss Beatrice nodded. "This way," she said, leading us from the bar toward a back hallway.

We headed down the narrow hallway where the offices were located. In the distance, we heard a loud clatter.

"Maddie! Run!" Nate's voice echoed from somewhere ahead of us.

Miss Beatrice led us forward and pushed open the door to the men's locker room. Inside, two men were feasting on the remains of a third man. They barely looked up at us when we entered.

Miss Beatrice dropped her knife. It fell to the floor with a clatter. "Allen?" she whispered.

I looked at the men. I vaguely recognized the man who must have been her boyfriend. I'd seen their photo together in the newspaper once before. The paper had done a write-up on his golfing success. Both men looked away from us and turned back to the bloody corpse, gorging on the flesh once more.

"Allen?"

Slowly, we stepped back.

"Come away," Logan said softly to Miss Beatrice, taking her gently by the arm.

"Allen?" she whispered again, but it was clear from the expression on her face that she realized Allen was gone.

In the distance, we heard a scream.

"That was Madison," Brianna said.

"This way," Brian said, moving toward an exit sign. At the end of the hall, he pushed open a door that led back to the reception area. Nate and Madison rushed down the hallway toward us.

"Fuck," Nate yelled. "Our parents are all fucked up. My mom bit Maddie. Maddie, you okay? Maddie? We need to get out of here!"

We raced across the room and pushed open the door. Standing right outside was a hulking man wearing golfing pants and a bloody polo shirt. He turned and looked at us.

"Go," Zoey said. "Get to the van!" She then lifted her gun and fired. The man's body rocked as he took bullet after bullet to the chest, but still he kept coming.

"He's not stopping!" Zoey said.

The man reached out for us, but Brian moved in and swung hard, cracking the man on the side of the head with the baseball bat. He went down.

"Go, let's go," Brian said, and we all rushed toward the van.

Zoey jumped into the driver's seat. Miss Beatrice crawled into the passenger seat alongside her. I slipped into the back and slid the door shut. I stared out the window in disbelief. The world was falling apart. The darkness in the world was consuming us, and now we were consuming one another.

CHAPTER
ELEVEN

"AHH," MADISON SCREAMED. "IT HURTS!"

Zoey flipped open the center console and pushed a medicine kit at me.

"Here," Miss Beatrice said, taking Maddie's hand. She opened up a bottled water and dumped it over the wound, revealing the bite mark.

I opened the kit. Inside, I found medical gloves which I pulled on. Healer or no, I was still my mother's daughter. No way in hell I was going to touch some weird contaminant.

The bite looked bad. I ripped open the small bottle of hydrogen peroxide and dumped it on the wound.

Madison screamed.

"Hold still," Nate yelled at her.

"I'm so sorry, Madison. Please, let me clean it and bandage it up. I'm so sorry, but we need to get the germs out," I told her.

Madison cried, shaking her head, but didn't answer.

I pulled out an alcohol wipe and worked the wound while trying to see the injury in more ways than one. The aura all around Madison's arm was confused. It was like a tornado of blackness was sweeping across her, dimming the yellow light the made the halo around the rest of her body.

I quickly applied the cream and started bandaging her up as Zoey sped away from the country club and out of town.

Two police cars whipped past, sirens blasting.

"Madison, be still for just a minute," I told her then rested her arm gently on my leg.

I rubbed my hands together, envisioning them surrounded with a rainbow of light, then went after the darkness that was slowly creeping up her arm.

"What are you doing?" Nate asked in an accusatory tone.

"I'm trying to heal her. Shut up so I can focus," I replied.

"Witchcraft? Don't use witchcraft on my sister!"

Madison groaned.

"Be quiet," I scolded him. I pulled at the black energy that snaked around her arm and up her body, but I couldn't get it off. It was stuck to her with long tendrils, just like Mom's headache. The moment I snatched at the dark light, it snapped back. "Dammit," I whispered. "It's not working."

"Where are we going?" Miss Beatrice asked.

"Witch Wood Estate," Zoey answered.

I pulled my hands back and smiled softly at Madison. "Just try to relax," I told her. "We'll get you some help."

Even as I said the words, I could feel something was wrong. The black energy was swirling like a tornado around her, swallowing up her light.

Zoey's van sped down the dirt road through the woods. We road in silence as Madison groaned in pain. After a while, however, she became really quiet.

"Maddie?" Nate whispered. "Amelia, I think she's unconscious," he said aghast.

I put my still-gloved finger against her throat. I felt a pulse. "She has a pulse. Pain must have been too much," I said.

"Amelia, where is the gate? Aren't we close?" Zoey called.

I looked out the front window. Thick mist had covered the road. It made it nearly impossible to see where we were. I eyed the tree line. I couldn't even see the rowan trees.

Before we could figure out how close we were, however, Zoey jammed the brakes. A second later, there was a loud thump as the van hit...something.

We all tumbled forward, Madison slumping over onto the floor.

"What the hell?" Brian called.

"I hit something. Someone. I hit someone," Zoey exclaimed then put the van into reverse. She pulled back far enough to reveal a body lying on the road. She put the van in park.

"Mister Sanders. He's Madame Knightly's neighbor," I said. I opened the door and got out, Logan following behind me.

"Mister Sanders?" I called, but he didn't move.

"Jesus, did I kill him? Amelia? He isn't dead, is he?"

Zoey got out, Miss Beatrice following her.

"Mister Sanders?" I called, crossing the road to stand near him. He wasn't moving, and his arm was jutting out at a weird angle.

I bent low, mindful that he might be sick, and reached out

with a gloved hand to shake his shoulder.

He groaned.

"Thank God," Zoey said then pulled out her phone. After a moment, she cursed. "No signal. What do we do?"

"We can't move him. His neck might be broken," Miss Beatrice said, then we all stilled as Mister Sanders' legs twitched.

"Mister Sanders? Sir, you've been in an accident," I said. "Don't try to get up."

Mister Sanders sat up slowly, and a moment later he turned and looked at us. His eyes were milky white.

At the same moment, I heard Brianna shout.

"Maddie! No," Brian cried.

Nate screamed a blood-curdling yell.

The back of Zoey's van opened and Brianna and Brian jumped out.

Inside the van, I saw Nate pushing his sister away as he tried to back out of the van. The dark aura had taken over her.

A gunshot startled me, and I turned back to see Zoey standing, legs astride, with her pistol in her hand. I looked down at Mister Sanders whose outstretched arm was reaching for me. She'd shot him in the head. He wasn't moving anymore.

Nate fell out of the van, Maddie jumping on top of him.

"No," Brian screamed, then kicked her off. But it was too late. Nate already had a massive wound on his shoulder.

"Maddie," Nate screamed. "Maddie! What in the hell did you do?"

The mist around the van swirled, a thick fog rolling in all around us. I could see the dense air moving, twisting between them and us.

I turned and looked at the tree line again. The grandfather oak that sat at the entrance to Witch Wood was just down the road, but the mist had completely enshrouded the property. The mansion wasn't visible through the fog.

"Brian," Brianna yelled as Madison moved toward him. Rushing forward, Brianna pushed Brian out of the way, half-stumbling as she slipped out of Madison's grasp.

"Zoey! Your gun," Brian screamed as he and Brianna ran toward us, Madison following quickly behind them.

Zoey raised her gun to shoot, but the trigger clicked. "Out of ammo!"

Logan, moving quickly, grabbed a large tree branch from the side of the road and swung it at Madison, but it only slowed her for a moment.

"Where's the gate, Amelia? Are we close?" Zoey asked.

"This way," I said, leading Zoey, Miss Beatrice, and the others toward the old oak. I found the tree easily enough, but the gate and the driveway were…gone.

"What the hell?" I whispered. I stood staring at the space where the gate should have been, but it wasn't there. And it wasn't just lost in the thick mist. It simply wasn't there.

"How far?" Zoey asked, looking down the road ahead of us.

I looked at the old tree. "It's here. It…it should be here. By the tree."

"What do you mean?" Zoey asked.

I glanced back at the others. The fog had enshrouded everything, confusing Madison who stumbled around like she was listening for us.

"Maddie! Maddie, why did you do this to me?" Nate whined

weakly then groaned in pain. I couldn't even see him through the thickening fog.

Looking back toward the place where the gate and fence should have been, I closed my eyes and concentrated, trying to see the gate with my mind's eye. I exhaled deeply, then felt for the gate. It was still there. I could feel it, I just couldn't see it. I took a couple of steps forward.

"Amelia?" a soft voice called from the fog.

"Madame Knightly?"

"Amelia," a soft voice called again. "Come."

I opened my eyes then squinted, focusing hard. A moment later, I could see the gate. It was vibrating in and out of view, but it was there.

"Hey, where'd she go?" I heard Zoey ask. "Amelia?"

"Amelia," I heard Madame Knightly call from the other side of the gate.

"Amelia? Zoey? Where are you?" Brian called. "I can't see anything." His voice sounded so far away.

I stepped toward the gate, focusing hard.

"Goddess, Mother, guide my hands.

Protect the innocent.

Bring them to shelter.

In peace and with thanks, I pray thee."

I reached out, and my hand connected with metal.

"Zoey," I called. "It's here."

"Amelia? Where are you? I can't see you anywhere!"

I could just make out her silhouette through the thick mist. "Walk forward," I called to her. The moment she was near, I leaned and grabbed her with one hand, not letting go of the gate with the other.

"What the…what the hell?" Zoey said as she eyed the gate. "How did we miss it?"

"The fog," I lied. Magic was at work here. The air all around us was alive with it.

"Logan? Miss Beatrice? Can you hear me? B. and B.?" I called.

"Amelia?" Miss Beatrice called back. She sounded close, but I couldn't see her. The fog was too dense.

"Amelia, come inside," Madame Knightly called from the other side of the gate.

"Guys, come toward my voice," I called. "Brianna? Where are you? Brian?"

Neither of the twins replied.

A moment later, Logan stepped out of the fog. He was leading Miss Beatrice. I breathed a sigh of relief.

"Brian? Brianna?" I called, but there was no answer.

"Can you open the gate?" Logan asked me.

I nodded and pushed the gate open. It released just enough to let us in, no more.

"Go ahead," I told him, motioning for him and Miss Beatrice, who looked pale and shaken, to enter.

Logan nodded then led her inside.

"Amelia?" Brian called, but his voice sounded so thin. It was like he was miles away.

"Brian? Bri?" Zoey called back. "I can't see them," she told me.

I shook my head and gazed all around. The fog was thick and charged with magic. It chilled my skin to goosebumps. We were in the midst of an enchantment. "Me either," I whispered.

"Amelia," I heard Madame Knightly call again. "Come inside. Close the gate."

"We should go back for them," Zoey said.

Everything in my heart agreed with her. They were my friends. I would never leave them behind, but my instincts urged the truth. There was no use. They were…gone. Or, perhaps more accurately, we were gone. "Madison is out there. And we can't see two feet in front of us," I said, but even I didn't buy the excuse.

"Brian! Brianna," Zoey screamed.

There was no reply.

"They're lost," Zoey said.

"Amelia, come inside. Close the gate," Madame Knightly called once more.

My heart slammed in my chest. "Brian?"

He didn't answer.

"Where did they go?" Zoey asked. "It's like they disappeared."

The mist had grown so dense that I couldn't see more than two feet in front of me. The fog swirled, moving like a living thing. My hair stood on edge as I felt the magical charge. Wherever Brian and Brianna were, there was no way we could find them now. "We need to go in," I whispered.

"You sure?" Zoey said, looking surprised.

I gazed out at the fog then realized, felt, what had happened. Witch Wood had protected itself, protected us. Brian and Brianna were lost to us. I just didn't know how to explain that to Zoey.

"We'll wait until the fog clears," I lied, hating myself for it, hating even more that my friends were out there, somewhere, and alone.

"Okay," Zoey said then went in through the gate.

I followed behind her, pushing the gate shut after I entered. When I turned to look at the others, I was surprised—and not so surprised—at what I saw.

Inside the gate, the sun was shining. There wasn't even a hint of mist in the air. The weather was calm, the rowan trees swaying in a soft breeze, their red berries hanging like ornaments amongst the green leaves. In the distance, I saw the familiar outline of the manor.

"Amelia," Zoey whispered, her eyes wide.

Miss Beatrice was wearing a similar shocked expression.

Logan, however, was wearing the oddest smile.

While I had expected to find Madame Knightly inside the gate, the only one waiting for me was Bastet who looked up with her twinkling green eyes and meowed.

EPILOGUE

Spring

I PUSHED THE WHEELBARROW PAST the hedge maze for what felt like the hundredth time that day. And just like the other times, I heard…something. Voices? Wind? I wasn't sure what. I stopped and adjusted my cloth hairband, mopping the sweat off my brow.

"Done already?" Miss Beatrice, who we'd all taken to calling Bea, asked. She was carrying a large tray of seedlings from the greenhouse toward the field.

"Almost. It will be dark soon anyway," I said. "Just came up for more lime."

She smiled at me. "Zoey has dinner ready. Better hurry up," she said then headed toward the south field where we'd been busy all day planting crops. Wheat, corn, potatoes, beats, tomatoes… we were growing it all. I only hoped that the crops would make it. We'd just about finished off the last of the supplies, and none of us had planned to head to town…at least not anytime soon.

I glanced inside the hedge maze. The foliage cast long

shadows. Mist swirled on the ground, blue light flickering off the leaves. I tilted my head to listen. I swore I could hear voices.

What had me even more on edge, however, was how odd Madame Knightly had been acting. It was like she was readying us for something. What? Why in the world were we spring cleaning every room in the house?

"Too much dust," she told us. "You'll all develop asthma."

Who were we to argue? Witch Wood had saved us and kept us safe all winter. None of us ever questioned how. We'd seen what had happened. We just didn't know how to explain it. What we did know, however, was that Witch Wood was safe...and we owed Madame Knightly.

I sighed then headed to the shed. Inside, I pulled the gasmask off the wall. It was the one Brian had left behind. The one and only time I'd gone outside the gate since the day the world ended, I'd gone out only briefly with Zoey to retrieve her van and my belongings.

What we found broke our hearts: Nate's mostly-eaten remains and Mister Sanders' decayed body. Zoey's battery had died so we'd pushed the van through the mist onto the property. There was no sign of Brianna, Brian, or Madison. They were just...gone. I prayed that wherever they were, Brian and Brianna were safe. And no matter how much I prayed, guilt still wracked me every time I thought of them.

Otherwise, for the past eight months, we'd neither seen nor heard anything. There was no TV, phone, radio, nothing. It was like the world had just stopped. So many times we'd discussed leaving Witch Wood to go looking for others, but we never left. We simply stayed put. Safe. After all, everyone we loved was gone: Logan's and Zoey's families. My mom. Bea's boyfriend. There was nothing outside the wall except death. And no one ever came looking for us…as far as we knew.

I pushed my shovel into the large bin of lime, adjusting the gas mask once more. The lime always made my nose itch and eyes water. Thankfully, the gas mask took the edge off.

I filled up the wheelbarrow and headed back across the lawn. It was dark now, but my eyes had adjusted to the light, and the moon was bright. It was too late to lime the field, but I could leave the wheel barrow in the greenhouse and pick up where I'd left off in the morning.

I pushed the wheelbarrow past the hedge but stopped when I heard something. This time, I was sure I heard voices. There was no doubt.

"This way," a male voice said.

My heart started slamming in my chest. How had someone gotten onto the property?

I heard a child crying.

"Almost there," the voice said once more.

I set the wheelbarrow down and picked up the shovel. It was too late to run. I'd have to face whoever they were alone.

A moment later, a tall man with dark hair came around the corner of the hedge. A red-haired woman followed behind him, holding hands with two small girls. A group clustered behind the man.

"What is it?" I heard a woman with a southern accent ask. She appeared from behind the man. Her long braid lay on her chest, and she was carrying an enormous wrench.

They all stopped when they saw me.

The man studied me, then said, "You don't need to wear that. The air isn't contaminated."

"I know," I said, pulling it off. "It's just for the lime."

"Where are we?" I heard someone ask, and from the back of the crowd emerged a woman with long, dark hair. She was carrying a sword. She turned to the man. "I need to go back now. How can I get back? Jamie…"

The man shook his head and gently set his hand on her shoulder. "First, we'll take shelter, decide what we can and should do," he said then turned to me. "You must be the ward. Is her majesty here?" he asked me.

"Her majesty? What…who are you people? How did you get onto the property?"

Just then, Bastet appeared from the darkness. The man's eyes went immediately to the cat, and he inclined his head.

"Your highness," he said.

I looked at Bastet.

What the hell?

But then I saw the aura around the cat shift, grow larger, brighter, until it flashed with blinding white light. A moment later, Bastet was gone and Madame Knightly stood beside me. She coughed lightly then adjusted her gown.

"Tristan," she said.

Shocked, I turned and looked at the group, my eyes meeting those of the dark-haired woman carrying the sword. She took a deep breath and stepped forward.

"I'm Layla," she said, nodding to Madame Knightly.

"I am Madame Knightly, and this is Amelia."

I turned and looked at Madame Knightly who was smiling at me.

"Uh…" I stammered, looking back at Layla. What in the world could I say? "Welcome," I said at last. "Welcome to Witch Wood."

THANK YOU

I hope you enjoyed *Witch Wood: A Harvesting Series Novella.*
If you would like updates about this series, information about
new releases, and free short stories, please join my mailing list:
http://eepurl.com/OSPDH

Thank you!

ABOUT THE WITCHING HOUR COLLECTION

Good witch. Bad witch. White magic. Black magic. Kitchen magic. Pick your potion. Ready for Halloween? The authors of the Blazing Indie Collective, who brought you the *Falling in Deep Collection*, are brewing up something new.

Check out all the novellas in *The Witching Hour Collection* coming October 2015:

Melanie Karsak: *Witch Wood*

Peggy Sue Martinez: *A Wee Bit of Magic*

Claire C Riley: *Raven's Cove*

Eli Constant: *Sleeping in the Forest of Shadows*

Margo Bond Collins: *Witches' Kiss*

Elizabeth Watasin: *Charm School: The Wrecking Faerie*

Erin Hayes: *I'd Rather be a Witch*

Carrie Wells: *Playing with Magic*

Evan Winters: *The Witch of Bracken's Hollow*

Minerva Lee: *Spun Gold*

Blaire Edens: *The Witch of Roan Mountain*

Poppy Lawless: *The Cupcake Witch*

Join our coven: Join *The Witching Hour Collection* Newsletter: http://eepurl.com/bdRtbD

ACKNOWLEDGEMENTS

With many thanks to Becky Stephens, Staci Hart, Nadege Richards, the Airship Stargazer Ground Crew, the Blazing Indie Collective, and my beloved family.

ABOUT MELANIE

Melanie Karsak is the author of the bestselling series The Airship Racing Chronicles, The Harvesting Series, and numerous other works. She grew up in rural northwestern Pennsylvania and earned a Master's degree in English from Gannon University.

A steampunk connoisseur, Shakespeare nerd, white elephant collector, and zombie whisperer, the author currently lives in Florida with her husband and two children. She is an Instructor of English at Eastern Florida State College.

Check out my amazon author page for other works!

Made in the USA
Lexington, KY
22 April 2017